ANNE MORICE

DEATH OF A GAY DOG

ANNE Morice, *née* Felicity Shaw, was born in Kent in 1916.

Her mother Muriel Rose was the natural daughter of Rebecca Gould and Charles Morice. Muriel Rose married a Kentish doctor, and they had a daughter, Elizabeth. Muriel Rose's three later daughters—Angela, Felicity and Yvonne—were fathered by playwright Frederick Lonsdale.

Felicity's older sister Angela became an actress, married actor and theatrical agent Robin Fox, and produced England's Fox acting dynasty, including her sons Edward and James and grandchildren Laurence, Jack, Emilia and Freddie.

Felicity went to work in the office of the GPO Film Unit. There Felicity met and married documentarian Alexander Shaw. They had three children and lived in various countries.

Felicity wrote two well-received novels in the 1950's, but did not publish again until successfully launching her Tessa Crichton mystery series in 1970, buying a house in Hambleden, near Henley-on-Thames, on the proceeds. Her last novel was published a year after her death at the age of seventy-three on May 18th, 1989.

BY ANNE MORICE

and available from Dean Street Press

1. *Death in the Grand Manor (1970)*
2. *Murder in Married Life (1971)*
3. *Death of a Gay Dog (1971)*
4. *Murder on French Leave (1972)*
5. *Death and the Dutiful Daughter (1973)*
6. *Death of a Heavenly Twin (1974)*
7. *Killing with Kindness (1974)*
8. *Nursery Tea and Poison (1975)*
9. *Death of a Wedding Guest (1976)*
10. *Murder in Mimicry (1977)*

ANNE MORICE

DEATH OF A GAY DOG

With an introduction and afterword by
Curtis Evans

DEAN STREET PRESS

Published by Dean Street Press 2021

First published in 1971 by Macmillan

Cover by DSP

ISBN 978 1 913527 95 2

www.deanstreetpress.co.uk

Introduction

By 1970 the Golden Age of detective fiction, which had dawned in splendor a half-century earlier in 1920, seemingly had sunk into shadow like the sun at eventide. There were still a few old bodies from those early, glittering days who practiced the fine art of finely clued murder, to be sure, but in most cases the hands of those murderously talented individuals were growing increasingly infirm. Queen of Crime Agatha Christie, now eighty years old, retained her bestselling status around the world, but surely no one could have deluded herself into thinking that the novel *Passenger to Frankfurt*, the author's 1970 "Christie for Christmas" (which publishers for want of a better word dubbed "an Extravaganza") was prime Christie—or, indeed, anything remotely close to it. Similarly, two other old crime masters, Americans John Dickson Carr and Ellery Queen (comparative striplings in their sixties), both published detective novels that year, but both books were notably weak efforts on their parts. Agatha Christie's American counterpart in terms of work productivity and worldwide sales, Erle Stanley Gardner, creator of Perry Mason, published nothing at all that year, having passed away in March at the age of eighty. Admittedly such old-timers as Rex Stout, Ngaio Marsh, Michael Innes and Gladys Mitchell were still playing the game with some of their old élan, but in truth their glory days had fallen behind them as well. Others, like Margery Allingham and John Street, had died within the last few years or, like Anthony Gilbert, Nicholas Blake, Leo Bruce and Christopher Bush, soon would expire or become debilitated. Decidedly in 1970—a year which saw the trials of the Manson family and the Chicago Seven, assorted bombings, kidnappings and plane hijackings by such terroristic entities as the Weathermen, the Red Army, the PLO and the FLQ, the American invasion of Cambodia and the Kent State shootings and the drug overdose deaths of Jimi Hendrix and Janis Joplin—leisure readers now more than ever stood in need of the intelligent escapism which classic crime fiction provided. Yet the old order in crime fiction, like that in world politics and society, seemed irrevocably to be washing away in a bloody tide of violent anarchy and all round uncouthness.

Or was it? Old values have a way of persisting. Even as the generation which produced the glorious detective fiction of the Golden Age finally began exiting the crime scene, a new generation of younger puzzle adepts had arisen, not to take the esteemed places of their elders, but to contribute their own worthy efforts to the rarefied field of fair play murder. Among these writers were P.D. James, Ruth Rendell, Emma Lathen, Patricia Moyes, H.R.F. Keating, Catherine Aird, Joyce Porter, Margaret Yorke, Elizabeth Lemarchand, Reginald Hill, Peter Lovesey and the author whom you are perusing now, Anne Morice (1916-1989). Morice, who like Yorke, Lovesey and Hill debuted as a mystery writer in 1970, was lavishly welcomed by critics in the United Kingdom (she was not published in the United States until 1974) upon the publication of her first mystery, *Death in the Grand Manor*, which suggestively and anachronistically was subtitled not an "extravaganza," but a novel of detection. Fittingly the book was lauded by no less than seemingly permanently retired Golden Age stalwarts Edmund Crispin and Francis Iles (aka Anthony Berkeley Cox). Crispin deemed Morice's debut puzzler "a charming whodunit . . . full of unforced buoyance" and prescribed it as a "remedy for existentialist gloom," while Iles, who would pass away at the age of seventy-seven less than six months after penning his review, found the novel a "most attractive lightweight," adding enthusiastically: "[E]ntertainingly written, it provides a modern version of the classical type of detective story. I was much taken with the cheerful young narrator . . . and I think most readers will feel the same way. Warmly recommended." Similarly, Maurice Richardson, who, although not a crime writer, had reviewed crime fiction for decades at the *London Observer*, lavished praise upon Morice's maiden mystery: "Entrancingly fresh and lively whodunit. . . . Excellent dialogue. . . . Much superior to the average effort to lighten the detective story."

With such a critical sendoff, it is no surprise that Anne Morice's crime fiction took flight on the wings of its bracing mirth. Over the next two decades twenty-five Anne Morice mysteries were published (the last of them posthumously), at the rate of one or two year. Twenty-three of these concerned the investigations of Tessa Crichton, a charming young actress who always manages to cross paths with murder, while two, written at the end of her career, detail cases of Detective Superintendent "Tubby" Wiseman. In 1976 Morice along with Margaret Yorke was chosen to become a member of Britain's prestigious Detection Club, preceding Ruth Rendell by a year, while in the 1980s her books were included in Bantam's superlative paperback "Murder Most British" series, which included luminaries from both present and past like Rendell, Yorke, Margery Allingham, Patricia Wentworth, Christianna Brand, Elizabeth Ferrars, Catherine Aird, Margaret Erskine, Marian Babson, Dorothy Simpson, June Thomson and last, but most certainly not least, the Queen of Crime herself, Agatha Christie. In 1974, when Morice's fifth Tessa Crichton detective novel, *Death of a Dutiful Daughter*, was picked up in the United States, the author's work again was received with acclaim, with reviewers emphasizing the author's cozy traditionalism (though the term "cozy" had not then come into common use in reference to traditional English and American mysteries). In his notice of Morice's *Death of a Wedding Guest* (1976), "Newgate Callendar" (aka classical music critic Harold C. Schoenberg), Seventies crime fiction reviewer for the *New York Times Book Review*, observed that "Morice is a traditionalist, and she has no surprises [in terms of subject matter] in her latest book. What she does have, as always, is a bright and amusing style . . . [and] a general air of sophisticated writing." Perhaps a couple of reviews from Middle America—where intense Anglophilia, the dogmatic pronouncements of Raymond Chandler and Edmund Wilson notwithstanding, still ran rampant among mystery readers—best indicate the cozy criminal appeal of Anne Morice:

> Anne Morice . . . acquired me as a fan when I read her "Death and the Dutiful Daughter." In this new novel, she did not disappoint me. The same appealing female detective, Tessa Crichton, solves the mysteries on her own, which is surprising in view of the fact that Tessa is actually not a detective, but a film actress. Tessa just seems to be at places where a murder occurs, and at the most unlikely places at that . . . this time at a garden fete on the estate of a millionaire tycoon. . . . The plot is well constructed; I must confess that I, like the police, had my suspect all picked out too. I was "dead" wrong (if you will excuse the expression) because my suspect was also murdered before not too many pages turned. . . . This is not a blood-curdling, chilling mystery; it is amusing and light, but Miss Morice writes in a

polished and intelligent manner, providing pleasure and entertainment. (Rose Levine Isaacson, review of *Death of a Heavenly Twin*, *Jackson Mississippi Clarion-Ledger*, 18 August 1974)

I like English mysteries because the victims are always rotten people who deserve to die. Anne Morice, like Ngaio Marsh et al., writes tongue in cheek but with great care. It is always a joy to read English at its glorious best. (Sally Edwards, "Ever-So British, This Tale," review of *Killing with Kindness*, *Charlotte North Carolina Observer*, 10 April 1975)

While it is true that Anne Morice's mysteries most frequently take place at country villages and estates, surely the quintessence of modern cozy mystery settings, there is a pleasing tartness to Tessa's narration and the brittle, epigrammatic dialogue which reminds me of the Golden Age Crime Queens (particularly Ngaio Marsh) and, to part from mystery for a moment, English playwright Noel Coward. Morice's books may be cozy but they most certainly are not cloying, nor are the sentiments which the characters express invariably "traditional." The author avoids any traces of soppiness or sentimentality and has a knack for clever turns of phrase which is characteristic of the bright young things of the Twenties and Thirties, the decades of her own youth. "Sackcloth and ashes would have been overdressing for the mood I had sunk into by then," Tessa reflects at one point in the novel *Death in the Grand Manor*. Never fear, however: nothing, not even the odd murder or two, keeps Tessa down in the dumps for long; and invariably she finds herself back on the trail of murder most foul, to the consternation of her handsome, debonair husband, Inspector Robin Price of Scotland Yard (whom she meets in the first novel in the series and has married by the second), and the exasperation of her amusingly eccentric and indolent playwright cousin, Toby Crichton, both of whom feature in almost all of the Tessa Crichton novels. Murder may not lastingly mar Tessa's equanimity, but she certainly takes her detection seriously.

Three decades now having passed since Anne Morice's crime novels were in print, fans of British mystery in both its classic and cozy forms should derive much pleasure in discovering (or rediscovering) her work in these new Dean Street Press editions and thereby passing time once again in that pleasant fictional English world where death affords us not emotional disturbance and distress but enjoyable and intelligent diversion.

Curtis Evans

One

(i)

'Well, Tessa! What would you say to a few days in the country?' Robin asked. 'Since that rotten old film doesn't look like getting off the ground just yet, it might be good for your morale to get out of London, for a bit.'

Some wives, I dare say, would take such proposals, out of the blue, with a grain of salt. Speaking as the wife of a C.I.D. detective, I took it with a spadeful:

'Rotten old crime being also at a standstill just now?' I inquired.

'Not exactly, no.'

'Then perhaps you have something special in mind?'

'Well, somewhere not too far away. We don't want to spend the whole time travelling, do we?'

'Oh, don't we?'

'Sussex might do. Somewhere near the Downs and a golf-course, and not too far from the sea. Do we know anyone who fits that bill?'

He was well aware that we did, and I was puzzled by the direction things were taking. It was beginning to sound as though he really did envisage a quiet, off-duty holiday, but I had still to be convinced of it.

'So what's Aunt Moo been up to?' I asked.

'Why nothing, I sincerely hope. Oh, I see what you mean! Yes, that might suit us splendidly. What's the name of her village?'

'Barley, to Aunt Moo. Spelt Burleigh and pronounced that way to all the rest of us.'

'Do you think she'd like to have us for a long week-end?'

'I could ask her.'

He was running his hand along the book-shelf where his road-maps were neatly stacked, and he pulled one out and spread it over the table behind the sofa where I was sitting.

'Burleigh . . . Burleigh . . . Yes, here we are! Inland, about twelve miles from Brighton; eighteen or so from Lewes. Just the thing. Could you try her now, or will she be at dinner?'

'I think I'd rather leave it till the morning.'

'Unlike you to throw away a chance to snatch up the telephone,' Robin remarked.

'Maybe, but I'd like to find out a bit more about this jaunt of ours, before I get involved up to my neck. Illumination may strike, if I hang on for a bit. Some of my best ideas come to me during the night.'

'That's true,' he admitted.

'And some of my best questions come to me during the evening. Like, for instance, what else is Burleigh near to, apart from Brighton and golf-courses?'

'Oh, it's a very posh neighbourhood. Bankers and stock-brokers thick on the ground.'

'And what is so appealing about them?'

'Well, for one thing, a good many go in for art collections, as a sideline.'

'So this is to be a culture holiday, is it?'

'In a sense. I imagine your Aunt Moo has the entree to all the best places, hasn't she?'

'If so, it could only be on her late husband's account. She wouldn't know a Leonardo from a Landseer. And what's behind this sudden interest in country-house collections?'

'I am curious to see if all the collections are in the right country houses.'

'At last!' I murmured, throwing myself back against the sofa. 'So we're getting to it at last!'

'Yes, we are, but there may easily be nothing in it, I promise you, darling. Just a little hunch of mine that I wouldn't mind following up. Shall I tell you?'

'What a question!'

'Well then,' he said, taking a pencil from his pocket and drawing a circle on the map, 'here we have a radius of twenty-five or thirty miles from Burleigh. There have been a series of art robberies over the past few months, all bearing the hallmark of the same organisation; and three of them occurred within the area I've marked.'

'What's so special about that? You said, yourself, that the district was stiff with tycoons.'

'I know, but there's an item in the evening paper which makes the coincidence a bit too large to swallow. If you ever read anything apart from the theatre reviews, you'd have seen it already. It's on the front page.'

I gathered up the newspaper, folded it into the right sequence and read out the headline: 'Half Million London Art Theft.'

'London?' I repeated.

'Just read on.'

I went through the first paragraph and looked up: 'I still don't get it, Robin. It says here that in the early hours of this morning thieves broke into the Mayfair home of Sir Maddox Brand, well-known art-expert and TV personality, currently on a goodwill visit to Moscow, and stole forty paintings valued at over half a million. Is he really a well-known TV personality? I've never even heard of him.'

'Then he can't be, can he?'

'Stop teasing, Robin. Is he?'

'Not necessarily. It's what they always say when they can't think of anything else, but I gather he's a minor celebrity. Anyway, stick to the point.'

'I'd be glad to, if I could discover what it was.'

'You'll find it right at the end. The news story is all in the first paragraph, naturally, but they've padded it out with some biographical bits and pieces. As you'll see, one of them refers to his so-called luxury Surrey mansion. Found it?'

'Yes, but we're in the wrong county.'

'Oh, that's another reporter's convention. "Luxury Surrey mansion" is no doubt a phrase which comes tripping off the typewriter all by itself, but this one happens to be in Sussex. It's a place called Haverfield Court, about four miles from Burleigh.'

'Oh, marvellous! Do you suppose he's the master mind behind the gang, and has now stolen his own pictures to put you off the scent?'

Robin laughed: 'If so, he can't have realised that he'd have you on his trail. Shall we go down and arrest him?'

'Yes, what fun! I'll chat him up in the rose garden while you sneak down to the cellar and check through the loot.'

'I don't know that it'll be quite so simple as that. Some rather unsensational spade-work may be required first.'

'Well, I hope you're not counting on Aunt Moo for that. I've already warned you about her aesthetic standards. She'll be able to tell you how much he pays the charwomen, and whether he has English or New Zealand lamb for Sunday lunch, but that's about all.'

'Never mind. It's all grist to the mill.'

'I beg your pardon!'

'I said it was all grist to the mill. It's an expression.'

'I know it is and it gives me an idea. What did you say this Surrey mansion was called?'

'Haverfield Court.'

'But that's where old Christabel Blake lives. Mill Cottage, Haverfield; just down the lane from the big house. Isn't that an amazing coincidence? Now, if there's anyone who is really well up in the art world, it's – Oh, Robin, you brute! How could you?'

'How could I what?'

'Lead me by the nose. It was Christabel you were after, all the time. Why not say so?'

'Oh,' he said cheerfully, 'it was much better that the suggestion should come from you. You always get so ratty when you think I am trying to use your friends to further my own ends.'

'I don't see why I should mind any less, simply because you further your own ends by trickery.'

'Well, never mind; I won't go near the old harpy, if you'd rather not. It isn't all that vital. Just a hunch of mine, as I told you. Come to that, we don't even have to go and stay with your aunt.'

'Oh, far be it from me to stand in the way of any hunch of yours,' I said, picking up the telephone. 'And, anyway, I wouldn't half mind seeing dotty old Christabel again.'

(ii)

Aunt Moo did not answer the telephone in person, ignorance of its mechanism being one of her devices for avoiding unnecessary exertion. On rare occasions she could be persuaded to speak a few words into the receiver, if it were placed in her soft white hand, but this was not one of them. Dolly, her factotum and scent-bottle washer, told me that she was watching show jumping on television. Between fences and thanks to a deal of cantering to and fro over the home course on the part of Dolly, we were able to establish that Aunt Moo would be glad to receive us at The Towers on Friday, provided we were prepared to take pot chance.

It sounded like a sinister proviso, but Aunt Moo's colloquialisms were invariably a fraction wide of the mark, and I requested Dolly to relay the news that pot chance would be the very thing.

'What sort of mood is she in?' I asked.

It was not an idle question, for, although very cowed in her presence, Dolly was always ready for a free and frank exchange of views about her employer behind her back, while prudently dissociating herself by phrasing them in the third person.

'A bit on the fidget, if you know what I mean, Miss Tess, dearie? Poor old Dolly was in hot water yesterday, when we found the sun had faded her bedroom curtains, but she's chirpy enough today. It'll brighten her up, having you and your boy here. She needs taking out of herself.'

I privately considered this to be a very slapdash diagnosis, because Aunt Moo had always achieved everything she wanted in life by staying rigidly within herself, but I promised we would do our best in that department, and preparations went forward accordingly.

One of the things I chiefly adore about Robin is his singular capacity to plunge headlong and immerse himself in each new project that comes along. It is like the Method, as applied to police work, and can be alarming to some people, because his manners, attitude of mind, even his appearance are tailored to fit each separate preoccupation, and they are never sure what to expect. Personally, I find it endearing, and I am not at all sure that it isn't three-quarters of the secret of his success.

Thus, having laid down the lines of his campaign to outwit the art thieves and having set the wheels in motion, he instantly began to think himself into the rôle of the deferential young man, setting forth to visit his wife's rich relations.

He smartened up his shoes and golf-clubs, debated with me at length about a suitable present for his hostess and spent a giddy half-hour at Simpsons, choosing an ice-blue pullover. The single imperfection in the last was the inevitable one that it looked too new, but we rumpled it up a bit and got the cat to sleep on it, and he declared himself satisfied. All seemed set for a delightful Sussex weekend.

(iii)

Strictly speaking, Aunt Moo, alias Muriel Hankinson, was not my aunt at all, being the widow and former housekeeper of my cousin Toby Crichton's great-uncle Andrew, on the distaff side. It was generally held in the family that Uncle Andrew's first wife had died of starvation, for his stinginess was legendary; but, if so, it may have been a broken heart which caused his own death a few years later, for Aunt Moo's character underwent some drastic changes as soon as the marriage contract was signed. Her interests remained firmly rooted in housekeeping and local gossip, but she acquired an accent of such strangulated gentility as to make her largely unintelligible to her former cronies, and her notions of austerity were represented by a sponge cake made with twelve, instead of twenty-four new-laid eggs.

At all events, this mean old uncle had not survived a minute longer than was necessary for Aunt Moo to get a tight hold on his every last penny, and her transition into opulent, domineering widowhood had been effected so smoothly that it seemed to most people to be the very rôle to which she had been born and for which all her previous life had been a mere apprenticeship.

Inevitably, her manners were not conducive to universal popularity, but she did possess one staunch champion in the person of my cousin Toby. No doubt his regard had originated in a congenital propensity to admire what others denigrated, but it had developed into a genuine affection, which, in a grudging way, was reciprocated by Aunt Moo.

Despite an age-gap of nearly forty years, they had much in common, being equally self-centred and equally reluctant to exert themselves when it could be avoided. Furthermore, their understanding may have gone deeper than this superficial level. Toby, for instance, had several times used some recognisable absurdity of Aunt Moo's for a character in one of his plays, but she had either not noticed this, or been secretly flattered by it. Certainly, she never scolded him, although other shortcomings, notably his self-indulgence and irresponsibility, received their full share of censure.

I referred to these matters as we drove through the interminable stretches of south-western suburbs the following Friday morning, for, although we both saw Toby whenever he was compelled to come to London, Robin had not set eyes on Aunt Moo since our wedding-day.

'In theory, she ought to approve of you,' I said. 'A fine upstanding fellow like you!'

'Not in practice?' he asked sadly.

'In practice, it entirely depends on how much you eat and how deliriously you rave about the food. You can lay the flattery on with shovels in that department. Hers is an appetite which grows by what it feeds on, in every sense of the phrase.'

'So we should keep quiet about the primary purpose of our visit? Let it be understood that it was brought on by a craving for hot dinners?'

'That will present no difficulties, as far as I am concerned, since I still don't really understand what our primary purpose is. Have you got your eye on someone in particular, or is it just a matter of spying out the Burleigh land and keeping an ear to the Burleigh ground?'

'That more or less covers it. I wouldn't object to a little heart-to-heart with Sir Maddox Brand, if the chance came my way. I hear he has now retreated from Moscow.'

'So you honestly think there may have been something bogus about that robbery?'

'No, I wouldn't go as far as that, and for God's sake, Tessa, don't go spreading the idea that I've suggested he's involved in anything illegal. The chances are a thousand to one that he's just another innocent victim.'

'Personally, I can never see the point of stealing valuable pictures. You can't sell them, you can't melt them down, and you can't even show them off to your friends. I suppose you could secrete them in some dungeon and prowl round in the small hours for a solitary gloat, but I should imagine that would soon pall, and the insurance would be such a worry.'

'Wherein, I may say you have touched on the nub.'

'Have I really? What makes the insurance bit so nubby?'

'Not in all cases, but in the particular series I'm dealing with three-quarters of the stolen property has been recovered intact, just before the insurance claim was due to be met.'

'How very fortunate! Perhaps the thieves found out you were on their trail and got the wind up?'

'No such luck. It was more likely all part of the original plan.'

'You mean some kind of practical joke?'

'Far from it. Quite large sums of money were involved; anything from five to twenty thousand pounds.'

I pondered on this, while Robin manoeuvred his way through the chaos of Streatham High Street. Then I said:

'The reward money?'

'Correct. Five per cent of the insured amount handed over to anyone with information leading to the recovery, etcetera. So up pops some innocent citizen, without the faintest whiff of a record, who's just had an urge to take a peep inside those crates which have mysteriously turned up in his barn or warehouse, or whatever, and just fancy!'

'A couple of million pounds worth of Impressionist paintings right on his doorstep, I suppose? All the same, Robin, however innocent this character may have seemed, he must, in fact, have been in on the racket.'

'Of course, but every life of crime has its humble beginnings, and he'd only have got a tiny whack for his part. Ninety-five per cent would have been paid over to the organisation, who never appear at all.'

'And the insurance companies play along?'

'Some do; and without too many questions asked. It's frowned on, naturally, but you can understand it from their point of view. There is nothing to link their informant with the actual robbery, and they only have to cough up a minute percentage of what they would otherwise stand to lose.'

'And it's your belief that there's a master mind directing operations?'

'It begins to look like it. And it's not a bad return, you know, for one night's work. The only risk is in the actual snatch, and the really tricky part usually comes after that, in finding a market for the loot. There are some other features, too, which set these apart from the routine jobs.'

'I thought there might be.'

'For one thing, a highly trained and discerning eye selects the pictures to be removed. Sometimes, from a whole roomful only one or two are taken. It appears to be a random choice, but it invariably turns out to be one an expert would have made. Then there's the packing and crating side. It's always done in a highly professional way, using methods which would be quite beyond the average burglar. Even after a lapse of months, the pictures are found to be in mint condition. So there you are! The owner gets his paintings back, the insurance company is let off lightly, and some happy little soul walks away with a few hundred in his pocket, to take the missus to the Costa Brava. Incidentally, Tessa, I begin to feel that we shall end up there, ourselves. Is there no end to this road?'

'You'll see a tree about four miles from here,' I told him. 'You can turn left there, if you like. Well, I should never be surprised if old Christabel were to come up with a few sidelights on all this. She's still very much in the thick of things, and I have a sneaking suspicion that she's not quite so dotty as she pretends.'

'That's good,' Robin said. 'No suspicions are too sneaking to be ignored on an expedition like this.'

Two

(i)

'If you plan to be around for a bit, Tessa, I might have a stab at painting you.'

'What's that you said?' I asked in some amazement, and Christabel repeated it.

It was not always easy to catch even the drift of her remarks because she invariably spoke out of one corner of her mouth with a cigarette dangling from the other, but on this occasion there was a further impediment to understanding. For the past few years, disdaining alike the counsel and cajolery of her friends and advisers, she had concentrated exclusively on abstract painting of the most uncompromising obscurity, and recognisable objects were a thing of the past.

Had I been Christabel, I should have applied my talents mainly to self-portraits. Although now ancient, raddled and unkempt, she still possessed the most stunning bone-structure I had ever seen outside an early Garbo movie, with luminous, deep-set eyes, undimmed by advancing myopia. I might add that this opinion had been endorsed by experts, too, because for twenty years she had been the sole model and mistress of an eminent old artist called Daniel Mott, who had bequeathed her an immense collection of his own works, completed or semi-completed throughout his life, but never put on view.

This had placed her in a commanding position in the art world, for she was constantly wooed by dealers and galleries to part with some of them, or lend them for exhibition. Certain unkind rumours had circulated at one time, to the effect that Daniel had not left her these pictures at all, but that during the last days, when she had ministered at his death bed, a plain van had darted back and forth on a succession of moonlight flits and conveyed them to a secret destination. However, I discounted them entirely, for poor old Christabel had not a particle of greed in her nature, as was evinced by her choosing the gypsy existence at Mill Cottage, when the sale of only one of Daniel's paintings would have kept her in luxury for years. Furthermore, although she had subsequently branched out and developed a considerable talent of her own, she had resolutely refused to commercialise it, devoting herself to these outlandish abstracts, which she admitted gave pleasure to no one but herself, and to herself only in their execution.

I reminded her of this, and she did not take it amiss but mumbled:

'I know, ducks. It's the only thing that grips me nowadays. Meant to keep on until I'd painted it out, even if it saw me out first, but the fact is I'm going blind.'

'I'm not surprised, after years of this sort of thing,' I said, glancing around at the vast collection of daubs which littered her attic studio.

'I've got an urge to try a few more faces, while I can still see them. Frankly, you're not my type; I can't do much with pretty faces, as a rule. They give me the feeling there's nothing left to bring out, if you get my meaning?'

'Not at all,' I assured her.

'No, you wouldn't understand; but there's something about that grey and brown thing you're wearing which appeals to me. There's a quietness about it. I do love people with that quality of stillness, don't you? You have traces of it yourself today.'

'So would anyone who had just spent twenty-four hours in the company of Aunt Moo,' I said, not best pleased to be saddled with this muted personality.

'Oh, she's quiet, too, in her way; though purposeful, you know. She sails serenely on, like a plushy trans-atlantic liner, but you wouldn't catch her putting in to the wrong port. How long are you staying?'

'I'm not sure. Until Robin has had enough, presumably.'

Christabel stubbed out her cigarette in a saucer already overflowing with soggy butt-ends, lit another, screwed up her eyes and studied my greyish-brown quietness through coils of greyish-brown smoke.

'Enough of what?'

'Oh, healthy exercise, four hearty meals a day. A short trip on a plushy trans-atlantic liner, in fact.'

'With a game of bridge before turning in?'

'Quite so. I'm told we're in for a bit of that tomorrow night. Not that either of us plays, but Robin rather wants . . . that is . . . we thought it might be fun to meet these Harper Barringtons. Do you know them? They live in something called The Maltings.'

'They're fairly new here, but I know them, yes.'

'That doesn't sound terribly enthusiastic.'

'It wasn't meant to. I can't really do with them, myself. They're culture climbers. Always asking my advice about what pictures to buy. "Buy any damn bloody thing that gives you pleasure to look at," I tell them. They don't go for that; they're vulgarians.'

'Aunt Moo is all for them, but that doesn't mean a thing. What sort of vulgar?'

'Every sort. He's brash and boastful and she tries to compensate by being pseudo-diffident.'

'Sounds heavenly. Who else will be there?'

'No idea, except there won't be anyone who isn't some kind of celebrity, however bogus. In fact, you'll quite likely meet my landlord. He's a great favourite and he gives them much better advice than I do. Always foisting some new genius on them, who's going to hit the jackpot in a couple of years. That's the kind of thing they like.'

'You mean old Sir Whatsit down the road? I thought he was in Russia?'

'So he was, but someone pinched his mouldy old pictures and he came scooting back, worse luck.'

'You can hardly blame him. Half a million pounds would be enough to light a fire under most people.'

'Oh, poppycock! I know 'em well and they're not worth a quarter of that. Either the Press added a couple of noughts, to make a good story, or else they were grossly over-insured.'

'You fascinate me,' I said truthfully. 'You really do. And I gather he's another you're not on the best of terms with?'

'He's hell, if you want to know. Tricky as they come. Life has certainly not been the same since my old landlord died and Brand bought up the property. I was a fool not to have nipped in ahead of him and got the freehold of this cottage, but I have a fatal tendency to let things slide, and the old man who owned it before was such a poppet; never a cross word. I just assumed that things would go on in the same way.'

'Haven't you got a lease?'

'Umm.'

'Then he can't turn you out?'

'He doesn't need to. He only has to sit tight and let the place fall down around me, which it's rapidly doing. The roof leaks, we're riddled with dry rot and he won't raise a finger.'

'Couldn't you do a few repairs on your own?'

'Can't afford to, my dear. At least, I'd scrape it up somehow, if he'd sell, but he's after bigger fish. He thinks that with me out of it he'd be able to hook them.'

'Surely he wouldn't get much for it, if it's as run down as you say?'

'Oh, the cottage is only a detail. He could spend a couple of thousand on putting it in order and sell out for ten times as much. It's the site which is worth such a packet. An acre of copse and paddock, with a stream running through it and seventeenth-century barn thrown in. Can't you see them queuing up?'

'But you mean to hang on, in spite of him?'

'You bet. I'd probably do it, anyway, just to annoy the old bastard, but the thing is it suits me. I was here ages before bloody old Brand took over, and I like it here. Besides, I'd never find anywhere half so good as the barn for storing

Dan's pictures. That's dry and solid enough, and it's all that matters. Now, about your portrait? Shall I have a bash?'

'If you like. Will it take ages?'

'God, no. I work very quickly, once I get going. I'll either finish it in three or four sessions, or I'll find it's no good and chuck it in.'

'I expect it'll be all right, then. If necessary, I could stay on for a few days, after Robin goes back to London. I'm supposed to be working, but we've got a stalemate at the moment. Our leading lady refuses to appear before the cameras until the director is sacked and vice versa.'

'Who'll win?'

'Oh, I think he will. She's pretty bucked with herself, but it's a minority view and if she hasn't climbed down by next week I have a feeling they'll cut their losses and get someone else for the part. Whichever way it goes it's likely to be a week or two before they get around to me again.'

'In that case, how about Monday for a sitting?'

'By all means,' I agreed. 'I shall feel I am beginning a whole new career in pictures.'

(ii)

Despite the earlier reservations, the charm of my grey-brown quietness began to grow on me as I dawdled along the bridle path which provided Mill Cottage's sole access to the main road. A decidedly flattering vision of the completed work floated into my head, a sort of cobwebby effect with me at the centre of it, a shadowy Madonna type, radiating all this terrific stillness. I saw, too, how quickly it could become a cult, and to the first daydream was added another showing the jostling crowds as they hurtled into the Tate to catch a glimpse of this celebrated portrait.

Robin had taken the car to the golf-course and I had intended to catch the bus back to Burleigh, but these delightful fantasies naturally slowed down my pace a little and I saw the green double-decker go sailing past, while I was still fifty yards from the end of the track.

However, my newly acquired serenity was not to be ruffled by so trifling a setback and I stood patiently by the road side, quietly thumbing a lift from the first comfortable-looking car that came along. It was lucky for me that Robin was not travelling close behind it, for he strongly disapproved of such practices, but I told myself that he would hardly expect me to slog the whole four miles back to Burleigh on foot. Furthermore, there was something so sedate and confidence-inspiring about this well-groomed motor-car that I did not falter, even when the driver pulled up with suspicious alacrity and promptly revealed himself to be a wolf in sheep's clothing, or, more literally, a wolf in a Rover. He must have been quite old, sixty at least, but was stunningly well set up, with gleaming black hair and gleaming teeth, not to mention a gleam in the eye signifying that all passion was far from spent.

It was a relief to discover, a moment later, that there was a granddaughter, or something of that category, buried under a fur rug in the back seat. Having stated my destination and accepted the driver's effusive invitation to hop in beside him, I swivelled round to address myself to this young person. She was about fifteen years old and the fur rug turned out to be a golden retriever, stretched out across the seat, with its head in her lap. Its one visible eye stared at me unwinkingly, overflowing with self-pity.

'What's his name?' I asked.

'Printh. Heeth hurt hith leg.'

She did not make a very good job of it, but her mouth was so full of brassware that it was quite an achievement to speak at all.

'What happened?'

'Thwath an athident.'

'Poor chap got run over,' the driver interposed. 'He'll be all right now, though. We've just been along to the vet to get the plastic splint off.'

I regretted his taking over the dialogue, as it would have been interesting to hear what the girl did with the last set of sibilants.

'If you could drop me at the crossroads,' I said, 'that would do fine. No need to go right into the village, if it's out of your way.'

'Oh, I think we should take our charming passenger right to her front door, don't you, Annie?' this flash Harry of a driver said, raising his silvery voice. 'Easy enough to go round by Burleigh, wouldn't you say?'

'Yethercorth,' she answered, doing her best.

I could have banged their heads together, because the last thing I desired was to be seen by Robin or Aunt Moo alighting from a perfect stranger's car, but the greyish-brown mood was still dominant and I quietly expressed my gratitude, while even more quietly working out the counter measures.

We swept through the village and, a few hundred yards beyond it, I said:

'Here we are! Just ahead, on the left.'

'Here?' he asked, sounding rather startled, and with good cause, for what I had taken to be a single building proved, as we drew level, to be one of those mean little cluster of dwellings which are often to be found on the outskirts of even the most self-consciously picturesque villages. It consisted of a flyblown sweet-shop, a barber and tobacconist and a red-brick Edwardian chapel.

'That's it,' I said firmly, opening the car door and not specifying which of these desirable residences was mine, 'and thanks for the lift.'

'It was a great pleasure, I assure you. Any time at all.'

I stood on the grass verge and flapped a hand at Annie, before turning away. It was perhaps natural for the driver to assume that, in asking to be dropped at this spot, we had actually overshot my real target and that I should begin walking back to it. In fact, The Towers still lay ahead, and it was this small miscalculation which revealed something more about my highway Don Juan than had been intended for my eyes. Glancing once again inside the car, I saw that he had turned round and had one arm outstretched over the back of the seat. He could, of course, have been caressing the dog, but his face was half-turned towards me and its expression was by no means one which is normally bestowed on the four-legged friends. It occurred to me that, if the girl were really his granddaughter, then what we had here was a right old incestuous grandpa.

Two minutes later the Rover started up and overtook me, but my greyish-brown outfit must have merged into the landscape, for neither occupant paid me any attention, and, by the time I had covered the few remaining yards, I was narcissistically hovering round the Tate Gallery again, to the exclusion of all other preoccupations.

(iii)

For all its pretentious name, Aunt Moo's residence was only a moderate-sized house, of the variety which has nowadays often been converted into flats or a maternity home. It stood about fifty yards back from the road, fronted by a manicured lawn and a circular gravel drive, and had a slightly larger and less formal garden behind. Its sole distinguishing feature was the quartet of squat, purposeless turrets with which, luckily for the present incumbent, some architectural maniac had adorned the roof. These had provided all the excuse she needed to discard the name of Cedar Lodge, which had been one of Uncle Andrew's devices for indicating the modesty of his establishment, and replace it with Burleigh Towers.

There were two cars in evidence as I trudged up the drive, a shabby old station-wagon and Aunt Moo's ancient but immaculate Austin Princess. Harbart, her chauffeur, was polishing up the chromium, a job which in fine weather constituted the major part of his day's work. On wet days the Princess was not allowed to be taken out, and he spent them inside the garage polishing up the engine.

It had not entered my mind to ask Aunt Moo to allow Harbart to drive me to Mill Cottage because, in the first place, she disapproved of Christabel and her hocus-pocus way of life; and, in the second, the Princess was never permitted to leave the tarmac and venture into country lanes.

The latter ban extended to the house, whence all trace of country lanes was rigorously excluded, and the sight of my dusty shoes tramping into the hall sent Dolly scuttling about like a terrified mouse.

'Oh dear, I'll just pop up and fetch your slippers, shall I? No, you stay where you are, there's a good girl. Dolly will see to it. Just let's get those muddy things off, shall we, before Auntie catches us? Which pair shall I bring down? Those pretty red ones?'

'No, the grey pair, please. Is Aunt Moo in the drawing-room?'

'That's right. I've just taken the sherry in. She's got company.'

'Anyone I know?' I asked, as Dolly came scampering down the stairs.

'Let me see, dear. It's Mrs Robinson; Zany, as they call her. Had they come, last time you were down?'

'No. At least, I think I'd have remembered the name.'

'It's Russian, you see. She's one of them Russian royalty that got away, oh years back it must be. She bought up Nicholls, the grocers, when the old man had his stroke. A year ago last July that would be. Doesn't time fly, though? Must be getting on for two years since you married your boy.'

It was rather impressive to be staying in a house where the groceries were personally delivered by a member of the Imperial Family, and I remarked on the fact, adding that it was small wonder that Aunt Moo brought out the sherry for her. Dolly quickly disillusioned me:

'Oh no, dear, we have to get everything from the Inter these days. Nicholls is one of them antique places now. Junk shop, as your Auntie calls it. Does well, too, I believe, though goodness knows who's got the money for that sort of thing in this day and age.'

'Aunt Moo, for one, presumably?'

'Well, dear, if you were to ask Dolly, I'd say she sells more than she buys. Bert's up and down there twice a week with some bit of china or glass that she's taken a fit in her head she's tired of. Then, half the time she forgets what she's sent, and there's old Dolly turning the house upside down to look for it. Goodness knows where it'll end.'

Bert being Dolly's name for Harbart, I could see there were real grounds for concern. If the Princess were being pressed into service, Aunt Moo's latest craze must have got a formidable grip. It was a breathtaking situation from every point of view because, although she had got her hands securely on the whole of Uncle Andrew's property, she had only been left a life interest in it and when that terminated every last teaspoon reverted to his watchful family. I reminded myself to ask Robin if she were not in fact liable to prosecution and imprisonment; but, being in the meantime agog to meet the Grand Duchess Zany, I put on my clean shoes and padded forth to the drawing-room.

I greeted Aunt Moo with a respectful peck and she commanded me to say Hahdidoo to Mrs Robinson.

She always addressed me as though I were four years old, a custom which I had bitterly resented at the age of fourteen, although now, pushing twenty-four, found rather endearing.

This drawing-room, which exactly reflected her style and taste, achieved in a masterly degree the feat of being neither fashionably period nor fashionably modern. The carpet was patterned with dollops of pink roses and the curtains were of heavy lilac brocade. Every flat surface was stuck all over with filigree, tortoiseshell and enamel knick knacks, and every inch of wall space festooned with watercolours, ornate mirrors and china plates clamped into brackets. There were even silver-framed photographs dotted about on the piano, which itself was draped in a fringed Spanish shawl.

Aunt Moo herself was handsomely decked out in beige silk, with several fat coils of pearls cascading over the front of it, and cut a regal figure. Conversely, her companion was much more my idea of a female grocer than a Russian aristocrat. She was quite old, sixty at least, solidly built, with streaky grey and orange hair, and dumpy legs encased in woollen stockings.

The initial disappointment was partially compensated for by the fact that Exeniah, as Aunt Moo called her, whether royal or not, was unmistakably Russian. She demonstrated this by peeling off phrases in French, whenever she thought it would give her an advantage, and also by the uninhibited way in which she flatly contradicted any views which conflicted with her own. In this department, she was evenly matched by Aunt Moo, who also permitted herself certain social privileges and was equally self-opinionated.

The subject of the current argument, which they were going at hammer and tongs, was a Chippendale mirror that Xenia was intending to bid for at a forthcoming sale. She had brought the catalogue, and the main point of conflict was the price it would fetch at auction. Aunt Moo put this around the three-fifty mark, whereas Xenia, with many a 'ma chère' and 'dis done', placed it at twice that figure.

Luckily for them both, my greyish-brown mood was still in control and I was content to sit back and sip my sherry in silent, sweet tranquillity. However, as the battle thundered on, I was alerted by the name of Sir Maddox Brand being flung into the arena and, with a revival of interest, discovered that the twin brother to this mirror was to be found at Haverfield Court.

Anything pertaining to this character being what Robin called grist to his mill, I was enchanted to learn that Sir Maddox had as good as admitted to Aunt Moo that his own specimen was somewhat dubious. It had been knocked together, so he claimed, by some skilled operators in a London basement and was no more authentic Chippendale than Xenia herself.

Surprisingly enough, this disclosure brought an immediate cessation to hostilities, and Xenia proclaimed herself only too ready to believe it, holding the lowest possible opinion of Sir Maddox's integrity. She begged Aunt Moo for the details, beginning, if possible, with the name and address of these shady merchants. I regarded this as a smart move on her part, as she stood not only to gain some scandalous information about an important neighbour, but also the means to get some fake Chippendales run up for herself, should the need arise. However, before any more data could come my way we were joined by Robin, very fetching in the blue pullover, and Aunt Moo adopted a different manner in the presence of beautiful young men. Playing up nobly, he bent over her hand with a courtly bow, which I had not even known was in his repertoire. She asked him if he had done some nice golfing and ordered me to pour his gin and bittahs.

On the other hand, even this mellow mood brought no relaxation of the ban on smoking in the drawing-room, and as soon as I saw the cigarette case emerge from his pocket I whipped him out of the room, on the pretext of taking a stroll in the garden, to work up an appetite for lunch.

'We don't want to undo all your good work with one false move,' I told him. 'Only Toby is occasionally allowed to smoke in there, and then only on sufferance. She keeps a silver crumb-tray at the ready, in case he drops ash on the carpet.'

'I wish Toby were here to give me a hand now,' he said despondently. 'It's such a chore trying to make out what she's talking about. Most of that bowing and scraping is simply to disguise the fact that I haven't understood the question.'

'Never mind, it goes down a treat. And I've got news for you. I picked up some interesting items about Sir You-Know-Who, while you were out doing your nice golfing.'

I repeated Christabel's remarks about the so-called half-million art-collection and then told him of the workshop for the assembly of fake furniture.

'So, one way and another,' I concluded, 'he is turning out to be a regular old swindler, which is very satisfactory.'

'My nice golfing wasn't entirely wasted, either,' Robin said.

'Oh? You played a good game?'

'One of my best. It so happened that I was golfing round the course with the Chief Constable, so it behoved me to be on my toes.'

'How brilliant of you to wangle that! Oh, I see! It was all part of the pre-arranged plan? Not just a lucky fluke?'

'Well, I was aware, of course, that you could handle the case quite adequately on your own, but I am all for giving you a helping hand, whenever the chance comes my way.'

He looked mildly put out when I did not respond with a stinging retort to this witticism, but I had omitted to tell him about my new quiet personality. I was about to bring him up to date on this development when Dolly came scuttling out with instructions from Aunt Moo to wash our hands for luncheon, and we obediently trotted after her into the house.

THREE

(i)

THE news that I was to sit for my portrait did not get a rapturous reception from Robin:

'She'll give you three vertical eyes and bathroom tiles for hair,' he complained. 'And we shan't know where on earth to hide it.'

'Oh, never fear, darling! Christabel is perfectly capable of painting conventionally when she puts her mind to it. She's done some stunning portraits in her time. It's only lately that she's become hooked on the abstracts.'

In the end it was agreed that we should make a joint descent on Mill Cottage on Sunday morning, so that Robin could inspect her work and also pin her down, in his efficient, masculine way, to the number of sittings she would need.

We found her drinking tea in the kitchen, watched over by two cats, who looked noticeably sleeker and better fed than she did herself. Instead of the usual squashy cigarette-pack she carried around, there was an equally squashy package of chewing-gum, and she explained that she was out of fags. Robin offered her the contents of his case, but she shook her head, saying that it would do her a power of good to give up smoking until the pubs opened.

'Rather careless of you to run out on a Sunday?' I suggested.

'Bloody careless, but I'm always doing it, and it so happens that I've been up half the night coping with the breakers and enterers.'

'You mean burglars?' Robin asked, looking round the kitchen. He sounded concerned but not much surprised, and, indeed, the state of the room, had it belonged to anyone else, could most easily have been accounted for by a gang of robbers having spent the previous three weeks camping out in it.

'Not here,' she replied. 'In the barn, where I keep all the Motts. Heard someone barging around in there at about three o'clock this morning. Went to have a look see, but they must have heard me and bolted.'

'Not the cats having a party?' I asked.

'No, both asleep on my bed, and the cats have been trained not to knock over pictures.'

'Did you notify the police?' Robin asked her.

'No. Don't mean to, either. Trampling over everything and asking a lot of fool questions. Anyway, I don't know what's been taken.'

'No one ever does. You shouldn't let that deter you. You'd be surprised by the number of people who telephone us three days later to say they've just noticed the grandfather clock is also missing.'

'No, I wouldn't, but this is different. There are a couple of hundred canvases out there, some I haven't looked at for years.'

'Valuable?'

'A good many are,' Christabel said, moodily sloshing more tea over her cup and saucer. 'None I'd want to lose, at any rate.'

'Insured?'

'Naturally. Same objection, though. I can't claim unless I know what's missing.'

'But, still, you should report it, you know. Both to the insurance company and the police. Breaking into someone else's property is an offence, whether there is intent to steal or not. You're certain someone did break in last night? The paintings couldn't have got knocked over any other way? Draught through a broken window, for instance?'

'There's only one window and it's not broken.'

'So how did they get in?'

'Through one of the doors, presumably.'

'How many of them?'

'Two.'

'Unlocked?'

'No.'

'Still locked when you went to investigate?'

'Yes.'

'Anyone else have keys?'

'Not that I knew of.'

'Look, Miss Blake, I'm on your side, you know. What actually did happen? You heard a noise, you believed it came from the barn? What kind of noise?'

'Crash bang.'

'So you got up and went over there? Did you see a light?'

'No.'

'And you didn't happen to hear a car or anything?'

'No. All pretty negative, isn't it? You can see why I wasn't keen to call a copper? The poor fellow would have no alternative but to write me off as an hysterical spinster.'

'It's possible that you underrate him. However, that's not our worry, is it?'

'What is our worry?'

'Well, would you have any objection to my going over there and having a scout round?'

Christabel got up and shambled over to the scullery door. She took a rusty iron key from a hook and handed it to him:

'That's the main door. Want me to show you the way?'

'I'll find it. Shan't be long.'

When he had gone, she flopped back in her chair and pulled a face at me:

'What's he after now?'

'Oh, footprints,' I said airily, 'tyre marks, Russian cigarette ash, all that kind of thing.'

'Well, he won't find them. How about trying a few poses, while he's out amusing himself? You can sit where you are; I don't need much of a light.'

She took a drawing-block and some crayons from the kitchen-table drawer and, placing the packet of chewing-gum by her right hand, made a series of rapid strokes and dashes, commanding me to turn my head this way and that, to look up and look down, lean forward and back, and all the while glaring at me like a housewife appraising the cod on a fishmonger's slab.

Every two minutes she ripped off the sketch, dropped it on the floor and started a fresh one, at the same time angrily cramming another piece of gum into her mouth.

'I thought the point of that stuff was to chew it for several hours?' I said.

'Daresay it is, but I hate the taste once the sugary bit's melted. And stop yattering, there's a good girl.'

I obediently summoned all the stillness at my command, giving it out again in great auras of greyish brown, which proved to be rather wearing and did not produce any noticeably inspiring effect on the artist. So I soon gave it up and allowed my thoughts to wander: 'Why won't he find them?' I asked.

'That's better,' Christabel said, peering at me intently. 'Take that prissy look off your face, relax a bit, and we might get somewhere. What did you say?'

'I said: why won't Robin find any of those things?'

'Simple reason they aren't there. This chap came on foot, and is a non-smoker, so my voices tell me. Did you know you had one eye smaller than the other?'

'I knew I had one bigger than the other, if that's what you mean. I'm told it's fairly common. Did your voices tell you what his name was?'

'Never you mind. I know what you're up to, my child. Everything I say will be taken down in that little head and passed on to another quarter. Hallo! Is that your beloved returning? I'd better stop this and give you both a drink. Only beer, I'm afraid. You can come and sit for me tomorrow.'

'How's it going?' Robin asked, replacing the key on its hook.

'Not bad. I might make a job of it, if Tessa will just sit still and stop looking eager. Otherwise, I know what this portrait is going to be called.'

'What?' I asked, keeping the eagerness out of it.

'Copper's Moll,' Christabel replied.

(ii)

'Funny coincidence, would you say?' I asked, as we drove back to The Towers.

'Which?'

'Your being down here to investigate one lot of burglaries and running slap into another?'

'And there the coincidence ends. Whatever tricks your quaint old lady is up to, taking the insurance company for a ride does not appear to be one of them.'

'Do you think it was genuine, or do you go for the repressed spinster bit?'

'I hoped you might have some views on that. Is it in character?'

'No. She may not have married; I really don't know about that, but I'd say she's lived one of the most unrepressed lives of any woman I know. Hysterical burglaries are not in her line at all. What would be the purpose, anyway?'

'To draw attention to herself. That's usually behind it.'

'She doesn't need to. She gets heaps of attention, as it is. And since she's falling over backwards to hush it up?'

'Nevertheless, we shouldn't have known about it if she hadn't told us.'

'The fact is, Robin, I think she had forgotten you were a policeman. Her mind was full of the subject when we arrived, and she started blabbing on about it, as one would, to the first person who dropped in. It was only when you began nagging her about reporting it that she got so cagey.'

'Yes, that's my reading, too. We were expected to commiserate, give some meaningless advice and then drop the subject. Whereas . . .'

'It suddenly came to her that she was dealing with the law. So what's the significance of that?'

'Either she did stage the burglary herself and your analysis is wrong, or else it was genuine and for some reason or other she knows more than she is prepared to tell. I incline to the latter, not only because you're often right about people, but also because of the evidence I found in the barn.'

'Then you're one up, because she was certain you wouldn't find any.'

'There was enough to show that somebody had recently been having a field day in there. Paintings chucked around all over the place; some in frames, some not. Presumably, whoever it was had been searching for something in particular, and in some haste too. It was quite a shambles. On the other hand, there was no dust on the canvases, so the chances are that it happened within the last twenty-four hours.'

'Which doesn't prove that she wasn't responsible.'

Robin said slowly: 'I think it goes some way to proving it. I am not sure what Daniel Mott's paintings are worth now, in terms of cash, but from what you've told me they have a very special value for Christabel. Somehow, I don't see her tossing them around like so many packets of cereal. Not unless she's a very much more mixed-up old kid than either of us imagine.'

'Very true. She told me that her main reason for clinging to the cottage was to have somewhere warm and dry to store the old man's pictures. It's a puzzle. Can you see how there might be any connection between this and the burglary at Sir Whatsit's flat?'

'Not a glimmer so far, but I'd love to know a little more about what actually happened last night.'

'Then I shall bend my mind to it. It shouldn't be too difficult to catch her off guard, as we chat our way through my sittings.'

'I wonder! She's no fool and she won't take kindly to cross-examinations, if I'm any judge. So watch your step, Moll, old girl.'

(iii)

Elsewhere, Robin's fairy godmother had gone into action on at least one of his wishes and when we reached The Towers we found my cousin Toby's old green Mercedes parked in the drive. Harbart was polishing up the windscreen.

'Makes a change?' I suggested. 'Has he come to stay, or just for lunch?'

'Couldn't say. He didn't bring no luggage, but you can't never tell with Mr Crichton. It's as the whim takes him. Could be here for an hour or two, could be for a month.'

It was a shrewd evaluation, although Toby looked permanent enough, when we tracked him down in Uncle Andrew's library, the one room in the house which was licensed for smoking. He was lying on a leather sofa, reading a bound volume of *Punch* for the year 1922.

'Some of these jokes are rather good,' he informed us. 'I am jotting down a few for my next script.'

'How is the mood just now?' I inquired, as we lit up. 'Are you here for an hour or a month?'

'Everything depends,' he replied grimly, 'On Mr and Mrs Spiral Staircase.'

Since Toby rarely achieved anything but the loosest approximation to people's names, I did not comment on this one, but asked him how it was that they were in a position to govern his movements.

'He is one of those Hollywood tycoons, as you may have gathered. All very well in his place, but unfortunately he is on a trip with lovely Mrs Staircase to my lovely country and is obsessed with the idea of visiting with me in my lovely home.'

'Very understandable, but will it be quite the same without the lovely host?'

'Yes, of course. He will fancy himself to be in the guest house. That sort of thing is quite commonplace in some parts of California, you know. I stayed with people for weeks on end, without actually coming face to face with them. I have instructed Mrs Parkes to provide them with all they need and to telephone me the minute they show signs of departure. I shall then bowl over and tell them goodbye.'

'You will have to tell the Harper Barringtons Hallo, this evening, however,' I warned him.

'I've heard about that, but hopes are soaring. Mrs Flippety Flop is a stickler for even numbers. When my auntie told her I was here, she said she would ring round and try to get an extra woman. I wouldn't imagine our extra women having sunk so low as to be available at this stage, would you?'

'I don't know her,' I said, 'or how many extra women she has at her beck and call, but I gather that much will depend on how famous she thinks you are. Next to even numbers, she dearly loves a celebrity.'

'I will gladly step down and let you go in my place,' Robin said. 'The more I hear of this creature, the more reluctant I am to eat her salt.'

'Nothing doing,' I told him. 'You are here to mix with the local art-loving gentry, and my spies tell me that the Harper Barringtons are at the hub of it.'

Toby dragged his eyes away from the cartoons of tweenies and flappers and regarded us both with a gleam of interest.

'What are you after?' he inquired. 'If I may be so quizzical? Some undiscovered Van Meegerens?'

'No, something much more villainous than that,' I said proudly. 'Robin has –'

'Don't be so daft,' he interrupted. 'I don't know if you're aware of it, Toby, but things go from bad to worse in our household. If Tessa had her way, we'd have dramas for breakfast, lunch, tea and dinner. I can't even spend a harmless weekend in the country, without the James Bond element creeping in.'

I could have provided him with a little between-meals drama on the spot, by rounding on him for his perfidy, but the quiet grey mood still predominated and I confined myself to the merest trace of a Mona Lisa smirk, which properly took the wind out of his sails and doubtless did more to arouse Toby's curiosity than the flaming outburst they may both have expected.

I administered a ladylike reproof, however, when Robin and I were alone, pointing out that on several occasions Toby's co-operation had proved invaluable and that he had once so far outstepped the bounds of discretion as to save my life.

'Oh, I know, and I apologise; at least, I suppose I do, but you should try to understand that this is something quite different. It's not a case at all, in the accepted sense. I'm simply hoping to pick up any scraps that come my way, and the only chance of getting anywhere in that game is to melt into the background. If it got about that I'm here in any sort of official capacity, I might just as well pack my bags and leave for all the good I'll do.'

'Well, Toby wouldn't give you away,' I said. 'At least, he wouldn't if you took him into your confidence. But you know how perverse he is, and if you pretend you're simply here to do some nice golfing he's quite capable of spreading it around that you're tracking a gang of crooks with headquarters in Mrs Harper Barrington's parlour.'

'He could be right, too. It would be an unlucky fluke?'

'Why? You don't mean you've found a link already?'

'No such luck, but there are rumours of mysteries surrounding these Harper Barringtons. For one thing, they appear to have sprung to fame and fortune practically overnight, which always raises a few queries.'

'Why should it, though?'

'Oh, I realise it happens every day in your profession, but why should a middle-aged man, who's been jogging along in the City for twenty years, suddenly branch out with a villa in the South of France, a couple of racehorses and all the other status symbols, not to mention a collection of valuable paintings?'

'Yes, it's interesting, I agree, but I imagine it does happen in the City, too. One super, smashing take-over and you're up there, in the Monets.'

'You may be right. Is that what you'll invest in, when you make your pile, Tessa?'

'Sure! Until that happy day, though, I intend to be an inspiration to the living artists.'

'Like Christabel?'

'She'll do for a start.'

'Well, I hope the next genius you inspire will see you in a slightly less insipid guise,' Robin remarked. 'I think one might soon tire of that governessy look we've been getting so much of, these past two days.'

Four

(i)

In staking his all on the integrity of extra women, Toby had underestimated the lengths to which Mrs Harper Barrington was prepared to go in her quest for even numbers. At ten minutes past five, when he was proclaiming himself to be out of the wood and revelling in anticipation of the fireside supper Dolly would serve to him, our hostess telephoned to say that, all her efforts to find him a partner having failed, she had arranged for her own daughter to join the party.

'What an extraordinary woman!' he remarked, sounding as much intrigued as cast down by this blow. 'Imagine hitting on such an obvious solution only at this stage! I wonder where her daughter usually has dinner? Really, I begin to feel quite titivated.'

'I feel the reverse,' Robin said.

Personally, I was indifferent. Safe in the grey-brown cocoon, I was able to view the foibles of mankind with a tolerant smile. Luckily, I had packed a moth-coloured chiffon evening dress, among several others, and, obeying instructions, followed Aunt Moo into the Princess at seven-thirty sharp, my hair pulled into the Madonna style, a dash of the enigmatic effect with the mascara, and a sweet smile playing round my unrouged lips.

None of this got me off to a very promising start with Aunt Moo, who not only pronounced the result to be rather dahdy, but asked me twice on the journey whether the puppy had got my tongue. Not content with this, she sailed into The Maltings, introducing me to one and all as her niece, who did cinema work.

'You must feel ever so weird without your tray of ice lollies,' Toby suggested, as he joined me by the fireplace, he and Robin having arrived hot on our heels.

'Just look at this lot,' I said, turning my back on the room and giving my attention to a massive display of invitation cards. There were at least twenty, several gilt-edged, too, although I noticed that the summons to a Harvest Supper and the British Legion Coffee Party had been shuffled in at the back for padding, whereas the Ambassador's Reception, well to the fore, was a week out of date.

Our hostess came up to say a few words of welcome and offer us both a vodkatini. She was a compact, dark woman, with hair swept round into a chignon behind her left ear, and bold eyes and hungry teeth. Altogether rather formidable, and we pretended to have been inspecting a framed snap-shot, which also played its modest part as a card propper. It depicted two children, a pretty boy of about ten, holding a cricket bat, and a girl, slightly older, with spindly legs and a heavy fringe.

'Perhaps you'd prefer gin and tonic, then? I'll get Roger to see to it. Oh yes, my two offspring! Jeremy's away at the moment; staying with some frantically rich chum whose father owns about half Northumberland. There'll be no holding him, my dear, when he gets back. Anabel's here, though. You'll meet her tonight.'

'Oh, good!' I said, smirking at Toby.

'That was taken ages ago, I hasten to add. She's sixteen now. Ghastly age, isn't it?'

I asked her if her son was still just as good looking, and she answered:

'Jerry? God, no! Hair down to his knees last time I saw him. The only thing he carries about now, my dear, is a guitar. Honestly, I do think Eton is the most ghastly school, don't you?'

It seemed only civil to agree and, finding herself *en rapport*, she went on:

'I mean, just because he took ten O Levels when he was fourteen, I really don't see that's any excuse to encourage him to behave like a complete layabout, do you?'

Toby agreed that it showed a certain perversity, and she said:

'To be utterly frank, if I had my way I'd send him to the local comprehensive, and no nonsense; but unfortunately they have these perfectly wretched labs and so forth, and everyone tells me he has the most fantastic future in science or something, so there's really not much one can do about it.'

'Very trying for you,' Toby said, 'but it must end some time.'

'Oh, my dear, not a chance in the world! His tutor tells me he'll simply walk into Balliol or whatever it is, so I'm afraid we've got years of it. However, all my friends tell me he has the most divine manners, so perhaps one should be thankful for small mercies.'

'What a gorgeous room this is,' I said, introducing a new topic, since we seemed to be coming perilously near to the end of Jeremy's shortcomings, and she snatched at it gratefully:

'My dear, you must be joking! When did you ever see anything so pretentious? I got a wildly expensive young man to do it, simply because everyone told me he was so marvellous, and I said to him: "My dear, this is just a humble little sixteenth-century manor-house, and that's exactly the way I want to keep it." I ask you! Just look at the way he's tarted it up! Unbelievable! Roger can't understand what I'm complaining about, but I do loathe what I call swank.'

'Still, it makes a perfect background for your pictures,' I said, hoping she might be equally forthcoming on this subject as well.

'Oh, those! Yes, I am a teeny bit proud of them. Did you happen to notice the Tapies in the hall? Roger simply won't allow me to hang them in here, but one or two people have been quite impressed. Not that I can claim any credit for that, my dear. I happened to have the greatest living expert to advise me. Have you met Sir Maddox Brand, by the way? He'll be here tonight and I know you'll absolutely adore him. My dear, if you ever contemplate investing in a picture, do let me persuade him to give you some advice. I know he sounds fearfully grand, but actually he's the most simple person who ever lived, and a terrific buddy. The children call him Uncle Mad, you'll be shocked to hear.'

'I am sorry he has usurped the title,' Toby said, when she had left us. 'Uncle Mad is what I feel I am going.'

I took in a survey of the room, to see what further splendours and miseries were in store for us, and noticed Aunt Moo talking to Xenia. They were bulging over opposite ends of a sofa, apparently continuing the wrangle where they had left off on Saturday. Robin was in conversation with a middle aged man with buck teeth, whose face was vaguely familiar. From the air of deep concentration with which he did not listen to a word Robin said, plus the way his back hair straggled over his collar, I concluded that I had probably seen his photograph in *Spotlight*. I discovered later that he was Guy Robinson, husband of Xenia, although he looked a good ten years her junior. The name meant nothing to me, but the actor impression persisted as the evening wore on. This was mainly because, although he rarely said anything noteworthy, almost all of it was expressed in one or other of his repertoire of funny accents.

Our host arrived with the gin and tonic. He was a breezy, moustachioed man, with hot red eyes and a rib digging manner:

'Here we are, then! Sorry you've been left out in the cold. Cheers! Jolly smashing you could both come. I say, what's the drill? Do we call you Miss Crichton, or Mrs Price?'

'Oh, Tessa, please!'

'Good show! Quite a boost for Burleigh, what! having you down here. My missus was onto it in a flash, when Mrs Hankinson dropped the word. "Must give a party for them," she said. "Something terribly quiet and simple." So that's what we've got. Hope you won't be bored. She can't stand anything grand, if you know what I mean. I say, do try one of these, what d'you call it, canapé things. The caviar is the real McCoy, I can vouch for that. Friend of ours has just got back from Russia with jars of the stuff. Do dig in.'

'That's the kind of friend to have,' I said, doing so.

'Yes, poor chap had rotten luck, though. Some of his most valuable pictures were stolen while he was out of the country. Bloody shame!'

'Foreign travel usually ends in some disaster of that kind,' Toby said gloomily.

'Oh, I wouldn't go so far as that, old boy. Matter of fact, Nancy and I did a cruise round the world last spring. Can't say I'd want to repeat it in a hurry; cost us three thousand smackers, for a start; but, by God, those chaps lay it on, you know.'

'Which chaps?' Toby asked, looking bemused.

'Fellows running the cruise. Slap up job. And the food! Never saw such quantities in your life. I brought one or two of the menus back. Show them to you, if you're interested. Make your hair curl.'

'That would be fascinating,' I said, forestalling whatever comment Toby had been about to make.

'Remind me to show you after dinner. 'Fraid you'll have to excuse me now. I see the great man has arrived. I'm glad you're going to meet him, he's a brilliant chap; a bit out of my class, I don't mind telling you.'

'I have met him,' I said, but too late, for Mr Harper Barrington had sped away to join his wife at the door.

'That won't get you out of anything, you know,' Toby warned me.

'But it's true; I have met him. He's a well-known TV personality and he drives around in a Rover, looking for pick-ups. Only you mustn't repeat the last bit to Robin.'

'I have a feeling I know that man,' Robin said, joining us at this moment. 'Who is he?'

'Tessa feels it, too. I do not, but I can tell you that he is called Sir Branksome Towers.'

'You may have seen his photograph in the papers lately,' I explained. 'In connection with a half-million-pound art-robbery.'

'Oh, is that who he is?' Robin muttered. 'For a moment I was reminded . . . Oh well, never mind. I hope you didn't drink any of that vodkatini?'

He was still studying Sir Maddox with the steely, narrowed eyes of the dedicated Inspector, who is temporarily baffled, and he added, 'It'll come to me, I dare say. You're looking a bit quinced, Toby.'

'Not at all. I'm enjoying every minute. I adore these people; they make me feel superior. It is quite intoxicating.'

He had no sooner uttered this simple confession than a minor social skirmish provided a further boost for his self-esteem. No one, I think, had been unaffected by the reverent welcome which Mrs Harper Barrington had accorded to

Sir Maddox Brand, and an awed silence had fallen over the room, as he accepted her homage. So we were all attentive witnesses to what occurred next.

'Blissful to see you, too, darling,' he announced in his mellow tones. 'And looking radiant as ever! But, my dear Nancy, whatever are we thinking of? Where has Christabel got to?'

'Christabel?' she repeated, stepping back a pace. 'Why? Has something happened to her?'

'Well, it looks suspiciously like it, since she seems to have vanished. I had the greatest difficulty in persuading her to come and now I am afraid she has given me the slip and gone home again. Isn't that typical?'

'I am sorry to be so frantically stupid,' Mrs Harper Barrington said, 'but I hadn't the remotest idea you were bringing her.'

'Don't reproach yourself, my darling girl. How could you have known? I would have rung you from the cottage, but the stupid creature refuses to have a telephone. I've offered a thousand times to put one in for her, but you know how mulish she is? I called there this evening, and there she was, out of cigarettes and quite alone, poor dear. I simply couldn't have it, and, remembering that you were at your wits' end for an extra woman tonight, I absolutely pushed her into the car, and here we are! At least, here we were. Oh well, perhaps she's changing her galoshes, or something. Be a dear boy, Roger, and go and see. And now, my darling, where's my delicious vodkatini? I hope you've made them exactly to instructions? I'm not drinking anything else these days, not a sip of anything except my vodka and vermouth. Well, Muriel! How nice to see you! And looking very stately! Shall I tell you about my lovely Leningrad?'

'Just a minute, Roger,' Mrs Harper Barrington called in a pent-up voice. 'While you're out there, please tell Anabel that she's to have her dinner upstairs, after all.'

Being a large man, her husband had been obliged to stoop, to pass through this humble, sixteenth-century manor-house doorway. Caught off balance, he straightened up a moment too soon and crashed his head on the solid oak beam which supported it. There was a long pause and then he slowly turned, his face purple and suffused, and tears of rage or pain welling in his eyes. He raised an arm, though whether to clutch his own head, or to strike his wife dead on the spot was never to be known. Before either could happen, he had to move aside to let Christabel through.

'Evening all,' she said grumpily. 'Brand insisted on bringing me, Nancy; so blame him, if it's thrown you out. Look what I found in the hall,' she added, dragging forward a shrinking figure in a frilly white dress, who hovered in the background. 'Too shy to come in by herself, apparently.'

'Oh, doh be tho thilly, Crithabel,' the creature said, scuffling her feet and exposing a mouthful of wire netting, as she broke into nervous giggles. 'Ath tho I'd be thy of my own parenth.'

(ii)

'Well, Price!' Christabel snapped, taking her hastily inserted place at the dinner table and speaking diagonally across it to Robin, who was on our hostess's left.

'You mean What Price, don't you?' Toby inquired, from his seat between Aunt Moo and Xenia.

'And no sauce from you, please, Crichton. I've got enough trouble, without that.'

'Price is such an awkward name,' I confided to my neighbour, who was Mr Robinson. 'People are always making puns with it. When Robin got his photograph in the papers for rounding up a gang of crooks, one of our friends called it the Fame of Price.'

'I say!' Mr Harper Barrington cut in from my right, incapable, apparently, of saying anything without first saying that he was going to say it. 'Is that what your husband does? Gangsters, thieves, all that caper?'

'Oh yes,' I said proudly, then remembering Robin's injunctions on secrecy I added: 'At least, he used to, but he's now switched to a completely different department.'

'Oh, really? Interesting, is it?'

'No, frightfully dull,' I replied, improvising wildly. 'Just boring routine. Things like malpractice and misappropriation. It's all mixed up with company law or something, which I don't understand a word of; although, of course, I'm mugging up on it, so that we have something to talk about in the evenings.'

'Shouldn't think he'd find much of that kind of thing in Burleigh. Rather a sleepy little place, actually.'

'Oh, but he's not here on a job. Whatever gave you that idea? This is a holiday. Even policemen have them sometimes, you know.'

'Ah! Yes, I expect they do. Fact is, I saw him playing golf with our local bigwig yesterday. Made me wonder.'

'Oh, that was purely a friendly game. They've known each other for years. As a matter of fact, he's Robin's godfather,' I said, going too far, as usual.

At the same moment, I began to be afraid that Robin had heard me, for in my eagerness I had protested a thought too loudly, and he is antipathetic to my occasional flights of fancy. I only ever indulge in them in a good cause, but am apt to be borne away, when they do occur.

Luckily, my host's attention was claimed at this point by Aunt Moo, on his right, with some searching questions about his sources of fresh asparagus in August. This led to a dissertation about the six new beds which his gardener had laid down, or it may have been built up, followed by some hair-curling statistics on the tonnage of asparagus which had been carried on the cruise.

His wife was less happily engaged at her end, for although she was valiantly harping away on the absurdity of owning four cars when she would have been perfectly happy to travel by bus, it was obvious that her heart was not in it. Clearly, the wound inflicted on her by the loss of her even numbers would never heal, so long as dinner lasted and the untidy evidence remained spread out before her. She kept switching venomous glances from Christabel, on Sir Maddox's right, to Anabel who had been placed one down from her presumably to punish them both for being present.

It was not a particularly effective war of nerves, however, because Christabel was too blind to be aware of it, and Anabel barely lifted her eyes from her plate, except to cast an occasional yearning glance in the direction of Sir Maddox, which he was not in a position to appreciate.

The dinner, although not on the lavish scale of a cruise ship, was substantial enough and was served by two stocky, black-eyed women, one circulating with the dishes and the other pouring wine. Sir Maddox curtly refused this, calling loudly for vodka.

'Never take wine after vodka,' he informed us. 'One must stick to it through thick and thin. It is the purest form of alcohol we have. I hope to convert you all to it, in time.'

'That you can never do,' Xenia said angrily. 'Vodka is for peasants to get drunk on, like pigs. The aristocrats of the old Russia never drank anything but French wine. My father had the most famous cellar in Kiev.'

'Please fetch the vodka, Dolores,' Mrs Harper Barrington said, using a careful Spanish pronunciation, which Anabel would have been even more at home in. 'It is in the drawing-room; the white bottle.'

'I am interested in what you say,' Toby remarked, turning to Xenia. 'I had been led to believe that vodka was the done thing in Russia.'

'Nothing correct is done in Russia now,' she informed him flatly. 'They are all pigs and peasants. I remember, when I was a child, how my papa would drink half a bottle of Napoleon brandy to himself, every evening.'

'No wonder it became so scarce!' he said, sounding impressed.

'All nonsense, my dear Xenia,' Sir Maddox cut in. 'As usual, you allow your extremely hazy memories of Russia to be coloured by the wildest imagination. I have been there rather more recently than you, to put it mildly. I might add that I was fortunate enough to be in a specially privileged position. I was quite free to move about as I wished, with a driver and interpreter always at my disposal and without the slightest hindrance from anyone. I came into contact with some of the most cultivated people you could wish to meet, and they one and all drank vodka. Furthermore, contrary to what certain clever people in this country had assured me, I saw very little drunkenness in the streets.'

'I think it must be more popular over here than we suppose,' Toby said thoughtfully. 'I see very little drunkenness in the streets, myself.'

Aunt Moo choose this opportunity to announce weightily that brandy and gin blew out the skin, but it was not so with beah.

Mr Robinson was the first to recover from this astute observation, whispering to me that he did not normally go in for funny stories about drunks, but felt constrained to tell me of an incident which had occurred while Larry was playing at the Haymarket. He followed this ominous introduction with an anecdote I had heard from my grandmother, although, presumably, in her day the protagonist had been Harry at the Lyceum. Luckily, the sweet Giaconda smile needed only the faintest touching-up to get me through the opening stages and, long before the climax was reached, a diversion occurred in the form of Dolores re-entering the room. She had a defeated look on her face and was pessimistically waving a bottle of lime juice.

'No, no, Dolores,' Mrs Harper Barrington wailed, 'not that one. The white bottle. The Strikninov.'

'Strikninov,' Xenia rumbled disgustedly. 'Who can drink such stuff? Do you have no Arsenikov?'

'Allow me to tell you,' Sir Maddox said, without pausing to hear whether she did or not, 'that Strikninov is the purest brand of vodka obtainable in this country. Not perfect, I grant you, but I am reliably informed that it has been distilled five times and kept in the cask for seven years.'

'Ha! Tant pis pour vous, alors. Every child knows that vodka must be distilled ten times, unless it will poison you.'

'Please?' Dolores said, in a hopeless voice.

'I'll fetch it, thall I? Anabel said, leaping up with such abandon that she knocked her own chair to the ground and dashed Mr Robinson's wine glass over the table in one fine sweep, before flying out of the room, apparently oblivious of the holocaust she had left behind.

'Clumsy girl!' her mother said. 'I apologise for my idiot child, Guy. I hope it hasn't gone on your suit? Maria! Put the potatoes down and fetch a cloth. At once, please! Honestly,

I simply can't think what I'm going to do with Anabel. The awkward age seems to go on and on. Oh, I see you've found the bottle, Anabel? That's very nice, so now sit down and eat your dinner and stop trying to draw attention to yourself.'

Ordinarily, I would have pitched headlong into the babble which then broke out round the table to smother this domestic fraças, but positive reactions of that kind were no longer in my nature, and I drifted gently into my shell, allowing others to flounder through as best they might. I was thus in a unique position to pick up all the various threads of chatter which wafted around my head and which included the following:

Roger Harper Barrington asked Aunt Moo whether she had ever considered changing her car for a more up-to-date model, urging her to blow the expense and get a Rolls, whenever she did so. She replied that she would be unlikely to contemplate such a move without Harbart's approval, as she did not believe in keeping a chauffeur in order to do the barking herself.

Guy Robinson said that, for no reason at all, he was irresistibly reminded of a screamingly funny remark which Noel had once made at a party and which made him laugh every time he thought of it, a claim which he then proceeded to substantiate.

Nancy Harper Barrington entreated Robin to assure her that he was not one of those fabulous bridge-players who were practically professionals, since she and Roger made it an absolute rule to limit the stakes to a pound a hundred. Robin replied that she had better count him out, a decision which I privately applauded, seeing that he had not played bridge since he left prep school, when the stakes had been limited to whipped-cream walnuts.

Sir Maddox, meanwhile, was extolling the wonders of the Hermitage to the table in general, soon provoking Xenia to the categorical statement that every single picture within its walls was a fake, all the originals having been sold by the Bolsheviks in 1917. For some reason, this announcement sent him into peals of laughter, although, oddly enough, Christabel was now the main target of his derision.

'Can we let her get away with such nonsense, Chrissie? Come along! Stand up for me, please!'

'I know nothing about it,' she replied in her most surly voice. 'Why should I? I've only been to Russia once in my life and the only thing I remember is the subway.'

'Oh, you're too modest, that's your trouble, my dear. It always was, if I remember.'

'Talking of Hermitages,' I said to my host, feeling a duty, for Robin's sake, not to let such a promising opening slip by, 'you seem to have quite a gallery here, yourself. Isn't that Dubuffet over the fireplace?'

'That? Oh yes, believe it is. Can't say I care much for it, but people in the know tell me I got it dirt cheap. You're pretty well up in this art lark, are you?'

'No, I'm terribly ignorant, but do tell me –'

'Unlike me,' Toby said. 'I know everything about art, except what I like. I got that from the back number of *Punch*,' he added, acknowledging my squeak of laughter. 'I can see it's going to be quite a goldmine.'

'Looks like you two have the advantage of me,' Guy told us, using the Texan drawl this time. 'I jes cain't seem to figure out this culture racket, doggone it. Mrs Robinson, now, she's different, but I guess you have to be born and bred in little old Yurrup to appreciate art. Take this here Dooboofay, ma'am, you were speaking of; jes don't mean a damn thing to me.'

Even Toby was silenced by this monologue, but Aunt Moo was rarely at a loss for the *mot juste*. She observed that buffets were all very well in their way, but they could give her a hot dinnah, any day of the week.

This provoked ringing laughter from Sir Maddox and, to signify her disapproval, Christabel ostentatiously turned her back on him and addressed herself to Anabel:

'How's poor old Prince coming along?'

Tears of gratitude filled Anabel's eyes for this kind attention, but unfortunately the shock of being spoken to in civil terms caused her to jab her spoon too violently into the *bomb surprise*. Whereupon, to the *surprise* of no one, it split in half and bombarded her frilly white lap.

So, in a sense, we were all back where we had started, with the merciful difference that Nancy chose to ignore the incident. She permitted herself one venomous glance in Anabel's direction then raised her eyebrows and escorted half the party out of the room.

(iii)

'Your husband tells me that neither of you is frantically keen on bridge,' Nancy said, when I had finished commiserating with her on the bad proportions of her bedroom and the many inconveniences attached to a sunken bath.

'But please don't let that spoil your game. We shall be quite happy to be left out, and we're dying to have a proper look at your pictures.'

'The trouble is that Christabel's being here has upset things completely. Don't get me wrong, my dear; I think she's a simply marvellous person, for her age, and I'd have invited her in the first place, if I'd known she was a friend of yours. But the poor old thing can hardly see the cards nowadays and it's a bit rough on her partners. If it wouldn't absolutely bore you to extinction, Roger thinks we should show one or two of the films he shot on our trip round the world.'

All my diligent practice with the saintly smile came in handy just then and I murmured that it would be delightful.

'But you would be utterly frank, my dear, and tell me if you simply hated the idea? One knows home movies are a bit of a joke, but Roger is so frightfully proud of his efforts and I must admit that one or two people we've shown them to have been absolutely stunned.'

'I know we shall be, too,' I assured her.

'He took some really fabulous views of the Angkor Wat. Admittedly, one could hardly fail with it, could one? You've been there, I expect?'

'No, never.'

'You know, in that case, my dear, I honestly think you ought to see this film. They laid on some dancers for us and it's really quite something. I can promise you'll be fascinated.'

'But I shan't, my dear, you know,' I confided to Christabel, during a quiet conference in the bathroom. 'For some reason, I only find places fascinating on the screen when I've seen them in real life. I go quite mad with excitement over a shot of Hyde Park, whereas the Red Square is just a drag. I can't understand why.'

'It won't make a damn bit of difference to me,' she replied. 'The Angkor Wat could just as well be Haverford Market Place for all I'll see of it. I've come without my distance glasses. That fool, Brand, dragged me out of the house in such a hurry that I picked up the wrong pair. Still, if we do have the Red Square, we'll get a few more rockets from Xenia, which may liven things up a bit. So typical of Nancy to invite her and Brand on the same evening.'

'Why did she, I wonder?'

'Because she's a bloody idiot and imagines that everyone else is just as impressed as she is by a pantomime emigre princess, believe it or not.'

'And do she and Maddox always have this slanging match when they meet?'

'Oh, it's six of one and half-dozen of the other. She quarrels with everyone and he goes out of his way to needle her. Also, she has a special grudge because he puts it around that she doesn't know the first thing about antiques, and the shop is just a cover up for some illegal practice.'

'True?'

'Shouldn't think so, but that's Brand all over. Never was such a mischief-maker.'

'Yes, I even noticed him trying to get a rise out of you.'

Christabel advanced on the mirror until her nose was practically touching it, then retreated abruptly as though taken aback by what she saw, which was small wonder. Her hair gave the impression that she had begun by building a bird's nest in it, but lost interest in the project half-way through.

'Oh, me,' she said vaguely. 'He doesn't bother me, any more than a wasp buzzing in my ear. He wants me out, as you know, but he won't succeed and that's all I care about. Just let them leave me in peace for my last few years, and they can all go to hell, as far as I'm concerned.'

Unaware of this modest ambition, our hostess tapped on the door and discreetly reminded us that we were hogging the bathroom.

'Such a bore, only having three,' she complained, as we emerged in a fluster. 'Honestly, this is the most vilely planned house I've ever lived in.'

*

Bearing Christabel's warning in mind, I was at my most circumspect when Sir Maddox approached me in the drawing-room, with his springy, youthful gait and a cup of coffee in each hand. It had struck me that there were enough cross-currents running through this gathering to trip us all up, without my charging the emotional atmosphere still further, and his arch expression put me still more on my guard.

Sure enough, he dropped straight into a corny, flirtatious banter:

'Well, well, what a mysterious little person it is, to be sure! I didn't recognise you at first. You look so demure tonight, one feels butter wouldn't melt in the mouth, but who could forget that lovely face for long?'

I had no idea who could, so kept the enigmatic smile in place.

'Though rather a prim face, just at the moment, if I may say so.'

There seemed no way of preventing him, since he had already said it, but, although he could not have been aware of it, he was treading on thin ice. My new look had already been described as govemessy and dowdy; and prim was no improvement. However, there was a growing risk that the epithet of crashing bore might be added to all the rest if I continued to cast my pearls before swine, so I aroused myself to a semblance of amiability:

'It was awfully kind of you to give me a lift and you may think I was purposely making some mystery out of where I was staying, but it wasn't like that at all.'

He took a gold case from his pocket, extracted a cigarette, lighted it from a giant, family-size Aladdin's lamp on the coffee table and then handed me the burning cigarette:

'You do smoke, I notice.'

'But you do not?' I asked, seeing no way of rejecting this gallantry without giving offence.

'No, never; although I am all for allowing my friends to go to perdition, in their own fashion.'

'Do you carry cigarettes around just for their benefit?'

'Oh, certainly. A lighter, too, as a rule, though I seem to have mislaid that. Does it surprise you?'

It left me totally and tremendously unmoved, as it happened, but still mindful of my p's and q's I simulated a mild curiosity.

'So now we are quits! You gave me a little riddle, the first time we met, and now I have retaliated. Can you think of a better start to a beautiful friendship?'

'No, I can't, but what riddle do you mean?' I asked, hoping the enigmatic smile might be coming up trumps, after all.

'The riddle of the damsel in distress, who was stopping at The Towers and didn't wish her Galahad to know. May he try and guess?'

'Yes, do, if you like, but I am afraid the answer is rather unpoetical.'

'Then would I be far out if I said that some rather prosaic family connection were involved?'

'Getting warm,' I told him, struggling to keep my end up in this idiotic game.

'Ah! Then may I just whisper what I think the explanation might be and you shall nod your head, if I am right?'

I reluctantly agreed and, leaning unpleasantly close, he murmured:

'Shall we say that you preferred to keep a certain relationship dark?'

I jerked back as sharply as though he had actually bitten my ear.

'Oh, no. At least, not if you mean what I think you mean. It was nothing like that at all.'

He smiled complacently, glancing across the room at Aunt Moo, who happened to be in earnest conversation with Guy Robinson. I could tell, from her graphic gestures and my own long familiarity with the theme, that she was telling him about her pearls, how much they had cost and how many of their brothers and sisters she had at home. The simple pleasure she derived from their possession was not the least endearing of her characteristics, but I had to admit there were times when the obsession could bring a blush to the cheeks of her nearest and dearest; and this was doubtless why I was quicker to take offence than the sneer really justified, when still smiling the all-knowing smile Sir Maddox said:

'A most estimable woman, no doubt, but a teeny bit of a joke in these parts, as you may have gathered. I am sure I don't know what we should all do without her, but one would hardly blame you for wishing to keep the connection quiet. However, I can assure you that no one who had met you could possibly conceive of there being any blood relationship.'

'Oh, that's a relief,' I said haughtily. 'You mean they would simply take me for the kind of vulgar snob who would accept somebody's hospitality and then cut them in public? Well, that is a weight off my mind, I must say.'

'Dear me! I have put my foot in it, haven't I? Then, may I ask: why all the mystery the other morning?'

'Yes, you may, but it was on account of quite a different relative. My husband, in fact. He has rather a phobia about my thumbing lifts and, since his job necessarily brings him into contact with undesirable types, that is quite understandable. I couldn't see your age, at that distance, and how was I to know what sort of a reputation you might have around here?'

So much for playing it cool! His insinuations had goaded me to the point where I had intended to be insulting, naturally, but the effect of my words was more electrifying than I had bargained for. White with anger, he said coldly:

'It seems that I was wrong in taking you to be of superior breeding to the comical old aunt. The similarities are quite marked, although she is at least an honest vulgarian; whereas you, you must allow me to tell you, are merely sly and pert.'

Whereupon he bade me good evening and walked away.

'I saw you having a terrific heart to heart with Maddox,' Nancy Harper Barrington said, unnerved, no doubt, by the sight of a guest sitting alone instead of decently paired off, and rushing in to fill the vacuum herself. 'Isn't he a charmer? You would never believe that a celebrated man like him could be so natural, would you?'

'No, it did surprise me a little,' I agreed.

'And I am sure you got on famously. Naughty old darling, he has a great eye for the pretty girls.'

'You don't say?'

'Oh well, it's not to be wondered at, is it? Those divine looks and fabulous charm! Women absolutely fling themselves at him. He literally has to fight them off.'

'And I am sure he does it most effectively.'

I believe she had been on the point of adding a further paragraph to the paeon, but something in my tone must have deterred her, and after a slight pause she reverted to an earlier theme:

'Roger is madly keen to have your professional opinion on his films. He's down in the cellar now, getting it all fixed up.'

'In the cellar?'

'Yes, we've made it into a kind of rumpus room; or fun room, as I prefer to call it. We got the idea from some darling friends of ours in the States, and I simply couldn't wait to get back here and pinch the idea. Adorable people called Jack and Connie Flatmore; do you know them?'

'No.'

'Oh, but, my dear, you should! If you ever go to America, I simply must give you an introduction. They have this fabulous Colonial-style house in Vermont, with simply masses of servants. I always feel so slummy when I come back here. But Roger has fitted out our fun room rather amusingly. He's got an extra projector, too; so at least one is spared that fiasco of the thing breaking down in the middle.'

I was sorry to hear this, having banked on the probability that it would break down in the middle, and was casting a gloomy eye at the Louis Seize clock, to assess the chances of getting away before midnight, when Anabel, having changed into dark blue jersey and slacks, sidled up to announce that Daddy was all thet and ready thoo thart.

(iv)

The Rumpus or Fun Room turned out to be a series of lavishly equipped apartments, covering an area as big as the ground floor of the house. There was a Hobbies Room full of photographic equipment, skewered butterflies and a model-railway track; leading out of this, a Games Room, with ping pong and bar billiards. The third and largest was the Projection Room, although at first sight it resembled a film set for a ducal library.

I do not know how far the guiding hand of the expensive young man had planted the finger of taste on it, but it did occur to me that the shelves of pristine volumes which lined the walls might have been bought by the yard, more for the harmony of their bindings than with the idea of pulling one down to read. It was not so, however, for, no sooner had we entered the room than Roger Harper Barrington pressed a switch and the section of shelves at one end of the room split into halves, swivelled round to reveal a white lining, and joined up again in the form of a cinema screen.

The gasps which greeted this transformation encouraged him to further magical feats and, one by one, the facades of books were peeled away to reveal the cocktail cabinets, record players and television sets which lurked behind them. I never discovered whether the room contained a single genuine book, but one tattered old tome which looked more promising than the rest had been hollowed out to make room for three decanters.

There were a dozen or so blue swivel armchairs set out on each side of a central aisle, facing the screen. Each pair was separated by several feet from the two in front, and had its own small table for glasses and ashtrays.

Aunt Moo plumped herself into the nearest available seat, just in front of the projector, and I took the one beside it. The Robinsons sat together on the same side, but three seats ahead of us Nancy manoeuvred herself and Sir Maddox into the pair which was on a level with them, on the other side; and Robin sat across the aisle from me and Aunt Moo.

Toby prowled restlessly up and down for a bit, before coming to roost in a chair midway between us and the Robinsons, and I knew that he was suffering from acute claustrophobia, among other afflictions. As soon as we were all assembled, Roger had closed the door leading to the staircase and freedom, and its rows of bookshelves had swung into line with those on the two adjoining walls. Toby found it painful enough to be enclosed in a sealed room;

and not even to be able to see where the door was situated must have been the supreme torture.

Anabel went importantly to a low stool beside a tape recorder just below the screen, a yard or two in front of her mother and her Uncle Mad, leaving only Christabel unaccounted for.

She had arrived after the rest of us, looking dazed and out of place in these chic surroundings, and stood hesitantly beside Roger, who was busy with his machines and paid no attention to her. She moved away from him and was about to sit down beside Robin when he raised his head, took in a comprehensive view of the room and called sharply:

'No, not there, Chrissie, old girl I Can't have that. I say, Nancy, would you mind swapping over and sitting with Mr Price?'

'Oh, certainly,' she replied, 'if you wish.'

'It's not me, old girl, but Christabel won't be able to see a damn thing up this end. Much better shove her up by the screen.'

Neither woman looked particularly entranced by the arrangement, but complied without argument and as soon as they were seated the lights went out.

Two seconds later, there was a warning shout from Nancy and they were switched on again. So engrossed had she been in chatting up Sir Maddox that it was only when thrust into the sobering company of Robin that she discovered that no one had anything to drink.

All three Harper Barringtons whirled around at top speed, to rectify this omission, until simultaneously stricken with paralysis by the discovery that the vodka bottle was once again absent.

I awarded low marks to Nancy for this oversight, and Sir Maddox called out with a trace of impatience that he could manage very well without it. However, Nancy would not allow this and insisted on making amends by fetching it herself. Possibly she had welcomed the excuse, for she was absent a good five minutes, which the rest of us fidgeted away, according to our individual natures.

Toby went on the prowl again, Robin sank into a doze and Christabel rudely swivelled her chair round, to turn her back on Sir Maddox and stare intently at the book-shelves on her other side, although I guessed that she could not even distinguish the mock titles.

Nancy returned, bearing a crystal jug containing the vodkatini mixture and a cut-glass tumbler, the latter causing Sir Maddox to break off his hideously boring monologue about a visit to some ghastly dacha, in order to express his admiration. This gave her the chance to moan a bit about its being the last of a set, and the hellish thing about servants being the way they smashed up one's few poor treasures, until Roger called for silence.

'Come on, now, troops, let's make a start, shall we? On your marks with the tapes, Anabel? Off we go, then.'

The lights went out again, the stirring notes of a sailors' hornpipe flooded the room and, simultaneously, the screen became afire with a brilliant extravaganza of colour, although so blurred as to have no outlines at all.

'Focus, focus!' Nancy bellowed, a split second after her husband had adjusted it and, as the picture cleared, we were introduced to a dramatic shipboard scene, with Nancy taking the principle rôle. This mainly required her to bare her teeth at the camera, which she stared at through jet-black sunglasses, while performing such breathtaking acts as lighting a cigarette, strolling to the side of the deck, to the sound accompaniment of 'A Life on the Ocean Wave', and waving her cocktail glass in a merry salute.

This opening sequence set the mood for the whole production and, as the minutes dragged by, we watched her emerging from the swimming-pool, studying the menu, laughing like a maniac at nothing at all and generally enjoying every minute of this mind-broadening voyage.

From time to time the gruelling monotony was broken by view of foreign ports, enabling Nancy to wear a succession of funny hats, often surrounded by colourful native characters selling their colourful native wares. Luckily, the tape recorder blared out a continuous selection of appropriate music, carefully edited to match each locale, which effectively smothered any yawning, groaning noises from audience, and there were two brief respites from the horror of it all. The first occurred when, contrary to Nancy's confident boast, the projector appeared to have broken down, after all. The humming behind my left shoulder ceased and the screen went blank. This time, Toby had collapsed into the arms of merciful oblivion and did not stir, but the Robinsons went into a short knock-about act in the aisle, in order, for some mysterious reason, to exchange seats. They had barely sorted themselves out into the new positions when Roger launched into reel two, on the second projector.

The other diversion arrived soon afterwards, when a fly staggered drunkenly from one side of the screen to the other, climbed slowly to the tip of Nancy's nose and remained suspended there. This brought piercing guffaws from Xenia, while Aunt Moo informed me that she would hate to go to Parshah and have insects crawling all over her. The rest of us, being more sophisticated types, pretended not to find it funny, and Roger, leaving the projector to whirr away on its own, strode up to the screen and flicked the fly away with his handkerchief.

We bade farewell to Nancy, at last, as the sun descended behind exotic Hong Kong, where the sampans plied their trade much as they had etcetera, and Anabel jumped up and switched on the lights. Various torpid forms jerked into life again and there was much blinking, murmuring and surreptitious consulting of watches, the quickest off the mark being Aunt Moo. With typical aplomb, she announced that Harbart's lumbago always played up to him late at night, and she would therefore take her leave. Only half a move behind, I leapt to my feet to insist on accompanying her and leaving the others to follow later.

Ignoring their dagger-like looks, as well as a fusillade of 'I say's' from Roger, who was already reloading the projector, I scuttled round the room, saying goodnight to everyone, in a fever of impatience to get away before Aunt Moo could be prevailed upon to change her mind.

There was a serious hitch when I got to Sir Maddox, because he was still slumped in his chair, perfectly inert, with his head turned away from me and I could not tell whether he was really asleep, or feigning it, so as to avoid a direct encounter.

As I stood hovering, I felt a sharp grip on my arm and the next moment Robin was tugging me towards the door. This was such a reversal of his former attitude that, although it suited my purpose, I could not restrain a polite inquiry as to what the hell he was up to.

'Shut up,' he growled. 'Cut out the questions, for once, there's a good girl, and get yourself and the old lady out of here as quick as you can.'

I can recognise an emergency as fast as the next person and, although seething with curiosity, bounded upstairs, bundled Aunt Moo into her sables and charged towards the front door. Nancy had followed, with Robin, to see us off and I begged her not to hold up the proceedings on our account. She obediently turned away, but as I drew back to let Aunt Moo pass I heard Robin say:

'I think they may have to be held up, all the same. Would you mind calling Anabel out? Ask her to telephone your doctor and to wait in the hall until he arrives.'

'Why?' she asked coldly, 'Aren't you feeling well?'

'Quite well, thank you, but I have to tell you that one of your guests is dead.'

FIVE

'IT DOES not surprise me in the least,' Toby insisted. 'Incarcerated in the bowels of the earth, deafened by palm-court orchestras and bored into solid stone, it was enough to kill anyone. When the lights went up I expected to be the only survivor.'

'I think we all did,' I agreed. 'And what made you so sure, Robin, that the old man wasn't in the same condition?'

'I knew it was the real thing,' he replied. 'I've seen too much of sudden death to be mistaken. There was something in his attitude. I confess I didn't notice it until you tried to say goodbye to him, and then the reflexes went into action, warning me to get my female relatives off the premises before anyone else caught on. It could only have been distressing for you and, naturally, at that stage I concluded he had died of a nice, tidy heart-attack, which, as Toby has pointed out, we were all rather prone to.'

This conversation took place in Uncle Andrew's library, where the three of us had adjourned when Robin and Toby returned from the Maltings. Aunt Moo had gone straight to bed, oblivious, as far as I could gauge, of the disaster which had befallen a fellow guest; and I had spent the long interval swallowing pints of black coffee and stamping up and down like a repentant suicide, an aching desire for sleep locked in deadly combat with my impatience to hear the grisly details.

'And hadn't he?' I demanded. 'Come on now, Robin! I'm in no state to prise it out of you by instalments. What did he die of?'

'It could have been self-administered.'

'There you go! What could?'

'Potassium cyanide.'

'Oh, crumbs! In the vodka?'

'Presumably. Unless he kept a cache in a hollowed-out tooth, like the war criminals. Anyway, they've removed the jug and glass for analysis, so we'll soon know. No switch was possible with either of them, luckily; they were both quite distinctive.'

'You mean the police have removed them?'

'Who else? Their own doctor came first and diagnosed death from unnatural causes. He refused to sign a certificate, so I rang the local branch. Superintendent Cole; nice fellow. He was inclined to be a bit old fashioned at first, on account of you and Aunt Moo not being available for questioning, but I explained how it was and he said he wouldn't bother you tonight, as it must be long past the old lady's bed-time. Very decent.'

'Very,' Toby agreed. 'And only wish it had occurred to me that it was long past mine. I find this kind of thing so unnerving. Even the dreaded Spirals couldn't have been worse.'

Robin said: 'It was Cole who tipped me off about the cyanide.'

'But none of the others know?'

'Except the murderer. That is, if there is one.'

'Certainly there is,' Toby said. 'And that's what I find so distressing; because I can name her. I would have told that cool confident Superintendent, if I hadn't been afraid of his making an arrest on the spot, which would have been rather more than I could have borne at that time of night.'

'You can tell me,' Robin said. 'I will promise not to go out and arrest anyone on the strength of it.'

'I am staggered that the trained mind should need telling. Remembering that Sir Brands Essence was a spy; for our side, I need hardly add . . .'

'How can we remember that, when we didn't know it?' I asked.

'Oh, going on and on like that about wonderful Russia. It's a dead giveaway, if you know anything about the world of espionage.'

'It's also a dead bore and I'm glad I don't move in it more often,' I remarked.

'So, accepting this extravagant premise, I suppose we designate Xenia the counter spy?' Robin asked with some amusement.

'Quite right, my dear. Taking the opposite line, you notice? All that fatuous talk about the Aristos practically proves her to be a Soviet spy. A very overdone performance, in my opinion. It certainly indicates that she would be quite incapable of perpetrating such a neat little murder.'

'I wouldn't be too sure of that, Toby. It could be the counter bluff, you know.'

'I have lost my bearings,' Robin complained. 'I thought it was Xenia's guilt that we were leading up to?'

'Dear me, no. I reject Tessa's suggestion absolutely. No, Christabel's your girl.'

'Can you be serious?' I screamed.

'You know he can't,' Robin said.

'Well, answer me this: who was sitting in pitch darkness, within inches of his glass, for forty-five minutes?'

'It wouldn't have needed forty-five minutes, or even forty-five seconds. And, if you're looking for opportunity, Nancy Harper Barrington had the best one of all.'

'That's true,' I agreed. 'She was out of the room for ages. That's when she must have done it.'

'You're forgetting that she had no desire to see him dead. She was probably the only one of us who felt any genuine regret for what had occurred.'

'I don't know, Toby. She might have been temporarily unhinged by his upsetting her even numbers. It is obviously a thing which goes very deep with her and she strikes me as a woman of strong passions.'

'His murder would have solved nothing,' Toby reminded me. 'With Sir Madcap gone, she was in an even sadder numerical fix.'

'Yes, I hadn't thought of that. It does rule her out, on the face of it? What about her husband, though? He had the whole room in view, all the time. He could easily have chosen the exact moment to drop a pill in the old man's drink. Yes, that's much more like it. What a pity! I quite like old Roger. He does so enjoy having lots of money; not like that twisted-up Nancy. Still, that must be the answer, you know. All that flashing about with the handkerchief, when he went to shoo the fly away, was just part of the legerdemain. An old conjuror's trick, in fact.'

'What about the old conjuror's motive?' Toby inquired politely.

'Well,' I said warily, 'There's Anabel.'

'So there is. What about her?'

'She could be the crux. A somewhat retarded adolescent, more than average mixed up, because her mother resents her. And why, I ask you, does her mother resent her?'

'Because she is plain and dull. I resent her myself.'

'Supposing there were more to it than that? A bit of the old Greek tragedy? What if Pa had an unnatural crush?'

Robin, who, to the casual observer, had been fast asleep, roused himself to say:

'We haven't all had your training in that department.'

'Besides,' Toby said, 'it has no significance. The breath of incest may blow through the Maltings, but no more gustily than in most well-conducted middle-class households. You would do better to stick to the facts.'

'But it is a fact that Sir Mad had been casting eyes at Anabel. Don't ask me how I know,' I added, casting a speculative one of my own at Robin. His eyes were shut again, but I had the impression that he was missing nothing, and I went on, after the barest pause:

'You will have to take my word for it. Furthermore, he got very uppish indeed when I put it to him that he probably had a stinking reputation in that department, so it's almost bound to be true.'

'I should think he might,' Toby remarked, 'whether it were true or not. It seems such a strange accusation to fling at a complete stranger, although I wish I had been there to hear it. My own conversations were so dull, by comparison.'

'Well, you have heard it now, which is almost as good because it brought our chat to a halt. But the point is that no one of his age would mind having the reputation of woman-chaser; he'd more likely be tickled pink; but chasing little girls is a different cup of tea and it certainly gives Roger a motive. Well, it's not perfect, I admit, but it makes him a much better candidate than Christabel. The idea of her doing such a thing is simply laughable.'

'What would you say if I told you I had actually seen her drop a pill in his glass?' Toby asked me.

'What could I say? I might try a few euphemisms but it would amount to the same thing.'

'Which was?'

'That you lied.'

He sighed: 'Correct. If you had believed me, it would have saved going into all the tedious details about motives.'

'I can see that does present certain difficulties.'

'Not the ones you think, though. It is more a question of *embarras de richesse.*'

'Indeed? Well, spill some of this *richesse.*'

'There are two obvious motives, although I haven't yet decided which finally goaded her into what I call the fatal deed; or whether it was a combination of both. In the first instance, we may as well assume that she was Sir Marketing Board's ex-mistress, not having forgiven him for discarding her.'

'May we?' Robin asked, unexpectedly bouncing back into the arena again and confirming my belief that caution should not be relaxed. 'And what evidence have we for doing any such thing?'

'No first hand evidence,' Toby replied. 'By which I mean that she hasn't told me so. I base my premise on the laws of probability, in which I may justly claim to be an expert.'

This was news to me and Robin did not even consider the announcement to be worth staying awake for, so Toby proceeded without interruption:

'Remembering that Christabel has had every art expert in Europe in her pocket, at one time or another, plus the fact which you have drawn our attention to that Sir Mad was a highly rampageous member of those circles, it is a fair bet, is it not, that they were once more than just good friends?'

'No, it isn't. For one thing, if she was such a nympho as you're trying to make out, why should one ex-lover bring out this hell-hath-no-fury strain any more than another? Furthermore, we all know that Mott was the one great love of her life, which completely ditches the whole argument.'

'Never mind,' he said cheerfully. 'Since you take that attitude. I'll try you on number two. Consider Christabel as the all time Soviet spy. I happen to know that she was a party member in her youth.'

'So were several thousand other people of her generation.'

'And it may surprise you to learn that some of them became Soviet spies. Not all those starry-eyed, left-wing intellectuals of the thirties saw the red light, if you'll forgive the amusing play on words. Some of them, as even you may know, are in Moscow at this moment. The laws of probability –'

'In which you may justly claim to be an expert –'

'Suggest that for every one who got caught there is at least half a one still at large and going about its business. I will swop Christabel for any two, dead or alive, that you care to name. It simply means that she is in the top bracket and clever as paint to have got away with it. Now, what more likely than that Sir Mad got wind of this when he was in Russia and was teasing her about it, which is precisely the way I interpret all those quizzical remarks of his at dinner.'

'I suppose it's logical, in a crazy sort of way, but I'm surprised at you, Toby, I really am. We know you must have your joke, and also that you're thoroughly unnerved by what's happened, but to pick on Christabel, of all people! You ought to be ashamed of yourself.'

Just for a moment he had the grace to look it; then he said in a low voice:

'Well, yes, perhaps I did get rather carried away, but I don't think Robin was listening, do you? And it's all conjecture, isn't it? I think one can safely assume that nothing has been said to give anyone grounds to go out and arrest anyone.'

'That's the first safe assumption that either of you has made, so far,' Robin said, yawning mightily, as he woke up for the last time.

He had underestimated us, however.

Six

I WAS awakened on Monday morning by Dolly summoning me to the telephone:

'I wouldn't have disturbed you for anything, dear, but it's one of those call-box places.'

Still half-asleep, I stumbled down to the hall. It was Christabel on the line, to cancel the sitting.

'Oh, why?' I asked stupidly. 'Isn't the fluence right?'

'No, I just don't happen to possess your divine egomania. Honestly, you remind me of Mott sometimes. It so happens that Superintendent Somebody or Other will be calling this morning, to ask a few more questions, or repeat the same questions; I'm not sure which. But, of course, you missed all that, didn't you? That's what comes of having a nice protective husband to ensure that your feet never actually touch the ground.'

'So it really did happen?' I said feebly. 'I'm sorry, Christabel, but I was only half-awake. Of course, I remember everything now. The Superintendent is coming to see us, too. What does he want to ask you about?'

'Whether I saw anyone lacing Brand's drink. What else?'

'And did you?'

'Wake up, child! Why would he be asking me all over again, if I had?'

'You mean he didn't believe you?'

'He didn't put it quite so bluntly, but I suppose that is what he meant. He said I might recall something when the shock had worn off.'

'I see. And has it worn off?'

'It was never on. He's wasting his time.'

'Still, you can't blame him for persevering. After all, he can't get many witnesses with such a close-up view of the event.'

'No, and too bad it happened to be me, wasn't it? Sharp-sightedness is not exactly my strong suit. Anyway, I can't stand in this capsule all day, talking to you about it. The point is that it's no good trying to think of work with this kind of thing hanging over one. Maybe tomorrow I'll feel differently. The idea of painting you is still hovering somewhere in the background.'

I went back to my room, just as Dolly staggered in with the breakfast tray. It was a sight to restore the sagging spirits, containing, among other delights, fresh raspberries, scrambled eggs and bacon, hot croissants and home-made jam.

'No papers?' I asked, rather ungraciously.

'They don't come Mondays, dear. It's one of Auntie's little savings. She says nothing much don't happen on a Sunday, except a lot of naked girls and traffic queues, so what's the good of throwing good money after bad on newspapers?'

'It is not infallible, however. Something did happen this Sunday.'

'Oh, you mean the poor gentleman passing on like that? Wasn't it shocking?'

'So you've heard about it already?'

'Your Robin told me, just before he went out. He is a thoughtful boy, that one. You're lucky there, you know. He said he was just telling me the sad news, so's I could break it very gentle to Mrs H., before she heard about it on her wireless or anything. Not that she's all that clever about turning the thing on by herself; usually has to call old Dolly to come and find the right station.'

'How did she take it?'

'Well, to tell you the truth, dearie, she said it must have been the shellfish you had in that pyelly rice thing. She said she didn't trust it.'

'The rest of us seem to be alive, though. However, she wasn't exactly knocked out by the news?'

'She'd heard it already, you see. That Zany rang her up at half-past eight, if you please, only two minutes after your boy had gone. Carrying on ever so hysterical, she was.'

I stepped aside from the main stream at this point to ask:

'Robin went out at half-past eight? That's a bit early for golf, isn't it?'

'Oh, he hasn't gone to play golf, dear. His clubs are all down in the hall. He's at the police station, over at Haverford. Can't keep away, I dare say. He told me I was to say when you woke up, if you ever did, he said, that was where you or Mr Toby would find him, if he was needed.'

However unwelcome the realisation that a murder or suicide had taken place in my presence, I was paradoxically annoyed that Robin had not woken me to report on his plans. It may not always be agreeable to be in them, but I do dislike being left out of things.

My two relatives were free from this persecution mania, and when I went downstairs an hour or so later I found them playing Beggar My Neighbour in front of the drawing-room fire.

'What's happening?' I asked, flopping moodily into an armchair and getting a cold glance from Aunt Moo for squashing up the mauve satin cushion.

'Momentous things,' Toby informed me. 'After a shaky start, Auntie has come storming back into the game and now holds three jacks, if I'm not mistaken. I am afraid my number is up.'

This dismal prophecy proved correct and, in three minutes flat, Aunt Moo had scooped the pack.

'Would you care to take a hand?' Toby asked me politely. 'It is quite *de rigueur* for three to play, so long as everyone is prepared for the game to go on for a fortnight.'

However, Aunt Moo told me that I could take her place, as she was off to the kitchen to knock up a souffle for luncheon, adding darkly that if Robin were late it would be his own watch-out.

'How about a stroll down to the village?' Toby asked, putting the cards away. 'We could buy some newspapers and secrete them in our bedrooms.'

'I wouldn't half mind. It's stifling in here; but you'd better go on your own. That Superintendent is supposed to be calling on me this morning, if he can tear himself away from Robin's company.'

'Ah! Then you haven't heard about your reprieve?'

'What reprieve?'

'Curious! There is something faintly disenchanted in your manner this morning and, knowing how public-spirited you are and all for the common weal, I had put it down to that. It just shows that one can't be right about people all the time.'

Perhaps this was his way of breaking the news to me gently and, if so, it succeeded.

'Does all this humorous chatter indicate that the Superintendent is not coming? Why not just say so?'

'How could I say so, when it wouldn't be true? He did come. Half an hour ago.'

'No one told me.'

'There was no need to. He asked Aunt Moo a few questions, and to say that her answers left him none the wiser would be the understatement of the century. Then he asked where you were.'

'I was in my room.'

'I know, and Aunt Moo explained that all you cinema workers kept very late hours, so he said he wouldn't disturb you, as it was doubtful if you could add anything to the existing confusion, or words to that effect. I detected a certain relief in his manner.'

'I can't see what reason there would have been for it.'

'Well, darling, not knowing about your being so public-spirited and mad for the common weal, he naturally concluded that you would regard his questions as a great bore, unpardonable infringement of privacy and so forth, which I believe is the line most people take. The fact is, he has fallen so heavily for Robin that he is scared to death of putting a foot wrong in that camp.'

'What camp? You seem to have very curious notions of what goes on in the police force,' I said crossly. 'Let me assure you that there is nothing at all of that kind.'

'Yes, you are in a mood, aren't you. Never mind! How about a little stroll, after all? Just time before the soufflé comes to the bubble, I should say.'

The painful sensation of being left out of things was growing more acute by the minute, and I resolved that Robin and his silly old Superintendent should rue the day when they had decided to plod on without my assistance.

'Okay,' I said. 'Why not? Let's go and call on the Harper Barringtons.'

'What a horrible idea! And I doubt if it would do us much good. Something tells me they only take the *Tatler* and the *Financial Times*.'

'I'm not talking about newspapers. I just thought it would be a constructive thing to do.'

'I am all for raising your spirits in any way that appeals to you, but is this quite the moment for a social call? There is bound to be a certain constraint after what happened last time they had guests in the house. There will be nervous tensions about, which is something I can't stand.'

'That's the whole point,' I said impatiently. 'This is not a social call. I simply want to find out whether one of them murdered Sir Maddox, and the tighter the tension the more chance of their betraying themselves.'

'Oh, well, that's different.'

'Naturally, we shan't let them see what we're up to. We shall make some plausible excuse for our visit. In fact, I have thought of one already.'

'Oh, good!'

'I shall say that you and I are planning a trip to the beach this afternoon and we thought it would be a friendly gesture to invite Anabel. They can hardly take that amiss.'

'On the contrary; they may take it so well that the offer will be accepted.'

'That's what we want, surely?'

'Oh, do we?'

'In that way, we shall edge ourselves into their confidence. We shall soon be in and out of the house, taking pot chance like old friends.'

'It sounds hideously boring and uncomfortable and I don't at all care for the way you are including me in this deathly programme. Why not leave all this sort of tiresome business to the police? Personally, I intend to ring up Mrs Parkes after lunch and see whether the Spearmints are on the move. If so, I shall not be going near a beach this afternoon, I promise you. I shall be beating my retreat.'

'I doubt if they'll let you. The trouble with leaving things to the police is that you have to play it their way. Naturally, you don't figure on my own list of suspects, but I've no doubt that, if you were to do a bunk this afternoon, they'd have the road blocks out for you all through Surrey and Berkshire.'

Privately, I considered this extremely unlikely, but I needed Toby as an ally and I was glad to see that my words had made an impression.

'So, you see,' I continued, driving home the attack, 'you'd do better to tag along with me. I don't anticipate needing more than a week to clear things up; after which, you can walk out of here, a free man.'

'Oh, very well,' he agreed reluctantly. 'Perhaps that would be best, but try not to spin it out. A week is really more than I can afford.'

There had been a certain bravado in setting this limit, but I airily assured him that a week would be ample, and I was very nearly right.

SEVEN

(i)

THINGS did not instantly fall into place, however, and the first to be out of it was two-thirds of the Harper Barrington family.

The door was opened to us by Maria, whose English was at least intelligible, although she seemed too bemused to take full advantage of it. By degrees, it emerged that Mrs Harper Barrington was in her room and would see no peoples; that Anabel had gone, but Maria was not knowing where; and that Mr Harper Barrington was inside, talking to policeman.

It was an impasse from which retreat seemed the only way, but just before Toby hustled me off the premises Roger's bellow was heard in the hall:

'I say, who is it now, Maria? If it's anyone from the newspapers, tell them no comment. Do it myself. Now, look here, chaps. . . . Great Scott, it's you, is it? Oh, good show! I say, do come along in and have a snort.'

'We don't wish to disturb you,' I said, amending the script a fraction. 'We just called to see if there was anything we could do.'

'You bet there is. Come and keep me company over a noggin. God, I need one, too. Up half the night with those police wallahs, and at eight o'clock this morning back they come! Gone to nose round the garden now; God knows what for. Nancy's just about flat on her back, I don't mind telling you. Now, what's it to be? Gin and ton.?'

Needing no pressing, I had galloped after him, followed at a snail's pace by Toby, and found myself in a trendy little room, with a glass and copper-plated bar in one corner.

'Gin and ton. would be gorgeous,' I said, hell-bent on ingratiating myself.

Roger was already at work behind the bar:

'No, I've got it! Much better idea. How about some champers? Got some already on the ice.'

'Oh, champers would be heavenly.'

'Good for you! It's some rather decent vintage stuff that I buy through a fellow at my club. I get twenty-four cases at a go. Works out a bit cheaper.'

'Oh, well, if we shan't be robbing you,' Toby said.

'No, no. Damn decent of you to drop in, specially after that shambles last night. God, what a thing to happen, though! Shouldn't have been surprised if you'd never wanted to set foot in the place again. Nancy says she wants to sell it and move right away somewhere. Hysterical nonsense, of course. She'll get over it.'

'I'm sorry she's taking it so hard,' I said, 'but I expect it's just shock and exhaustion, don't you?'

'Could be. Not like her to crack up, though. Strong as an ox, as a rule. Still, she's out for the count this time. Had to get our old quack to come and write a certificate saying she wasn't fit to answer any more questions. Don't think old Cole is exactly wagging his tail about it, but there you are! No point in paying through the nose to be a private patient, if you don't get some service out of it. And we can't have old Nance going off the rails. Anabel's bad enough.'

'What's the matter with Anabel?'

'Done a bunk, by the look of it. Lit out of here this morning, before any of us was up, and hasn't been seen since. Still, that's only to be expected. She's not a bit like her mother; goes to pieces at the drop of a hat.'

'It doesn't sound as though she takes after you, either?'

'What's that? Oh, see what you mean. No, she doesn't. And I'm not worried. Nancy's kicking up a fuss, but the silly kid will be back as soon as she feels peckish, I dare say. She's taken that damn dog with her, which is one consolation.'

'Don't you like him?' I asked. 'He struck me as quite a pleasant old party, in a maudlin sort of way.'

'You've seen him, have you?' Roger asked sharply.

What a mistake! To cover it, I said, prevaricating ever so slightly:

'Yes, for a moment. Last night, while you were all lingering over your port.'

'Good God! And I thought I'd got it through their heads that he was to be kept in his kennel. That's the trouble. He's not a bad fellow; the makings of quite a good gun-dog, in fact; but the women of this household make such an ass of him. Cosset him like some bloody lap-dog.'

There was an irritability in this outburst, which was such a marked falling-off from his former ebullience that I feared I had touched on a raw nerve. I was naturally all in favour of bruising as many of these as possible, but a dissertation on canine training did not promise anything very fruitful, and so, to get the adrenalin back in place, I swung round on a new tack:

'I do adore your bar,' I gushed. 'Don't you wish you had one like it, Toby? It's so absolutely marvellous and cute.'

Roger gaped at me for a moment, as though knocked off balance by the switch of topics, and then went into action again with the champagne bottle;

'That reminds me; time for a top-up.'

'No more, thank you,' Toby said firmly, setting his glass down. 'We're on a paper chase and it's time to move on to the next clue.'

'Clue?' Roger repeated in a distant voice; so I explained about the Hankinson phobia over Monday newspapers, and he said:

'Oh, good show, mustn't keep you, then. Nice of you to drop in. Let's hope they soon get this bloody business cleared up and then we'll have a real party, what?'

'So much for running in and out like old friends,' Toby remarked, as we retreated down the drive. 'Something tells me they are not quite ready for us yet.'

'It began well,' I said, glancing back over my shoulder in time to see some twitching of upstairs curtains, indicating that Nancy might have temporarily abandoned the horizontal position for a peek at the visitors. 'It was your talking about clues which scared them off.'

He shook his head: 'No, the freeze-up set in before that.'

'Anyway, it wasn't a wasted visit. We learnt a few things.'

'Such as the fact that he prefers dogs to be kept in their place. I can see that's going to be a big help.'

'Well, he sounded to me as though he wouldn't half mind having daughters kept in their place, too, wherever that may be. It rather puts paid to one of my theories. You could hardly say that he gave very strong indications of besotted fatherhood. But it was his account of Nancy's reactions which I found most fascinating. Why the total collapse? Does it mean that she was carrying the torch for Uncle Mad? She certainly burnt incense around him, but I assumed it was because he was the biggest lion in her zoo. Perhaps there was more to it than that? Do you suppose that Roger was the jealous husband and that what we have here is the straightforward *crime passionelle*?'

'No.'

'Oh, what a pity! I rather go for that.'

'Yes, I know all about your romantic tastes, and I hate to disillusion you but, in the first place, if there had been anything of that nature between Sir Brand and Nancy she'd have had more sense than to make such a fuss of him in public.'

'Not necessarily; but what about the second place?'

'I refuse to believe that husbands in Sussex go around murdering their wives' lovers. It would leave them practically no time for anything else.'

'You talk as though Sussex were some polygamous, offshore island. Besides, there has to be an exception to prove the rule.'

'This would be the exception to prove that he was off his head. Presumably, if you were planning such a risky deed, you would have to be an utter fool to choose the one moment when the three of you were locked up together in the presence of half a dozen witnesses, one of whom happened to be a detective from Scotland Yard. He would be in a first-rate position to find dozens of more favourable opportunities.'

'Which reminds me, Toby; whose idea was it to show the film? If you remember, we were originally invited to play bridge. It was only after dinner that the programme was switched.'

'I assume it was because Robin had made it clear that neither of you was in their class. And, of course, Christabel had upset the bridge cart, too. That was no part of the murderer's plan. Her presence was due purely to a last-minute whim on the part of the murderee.'

'All the same, I wonder if it was used as an excuse to get us all down into that dungeon? If so, it means that the murder was unpremeditated.'

'Oh, no. All the essential ingredients could have been present at the bridge table, too. With dummies wandering around and players swapping over, it would have been equally easy to arrange; easier, in a way.'

'Yes, I suppose you're right. It's not a profitable line of inquiry. Let's concentrate for a moment on Anabel. Can she have run away?'

'Can she? You sound hopeful about it, but I should have thought it would ruin all your plans?'

'Oh, they're elastic enough to take it; and it would certainly be damning evidence against Roger. I mean, if a sensitive teenage daughter had seen something to give her reason to believe that her father was a murderer, running away would be exactly the course she would adopt, wouldn't you say?'

'I don't know,' he replied. 'I only have one sensitive, teenage daughter, and I am not sure that she has ever considered herself to be in that situation. Can we go and get the papers now?'

The Maltings was less than ten minutes' walk from the village, so there was no reason to object. Moreover, I knew that he would be in no fit state for future collaboration, if he did not have his precious crossword to fall back on in moments of stress or boredom.

(ii)

I waited for him outside the newsagents, gazing down the village street, with its neo-Georgian banks and estate agencies competing valiantly with eye-catching multiple stores, including Dolly's Inter, where the insouciant manager doubtless cavorted around inside. Between its green and gold facade and Evans the chemist, directly opposite me, stood the bow-fronted shop which had once displayed the banner of Geo. Nicholls & Son, and whose cornflakes and soap powder had now been replaced by lustre jugs and warming-pans. On a swinging signboard above the door, the words 'Treasure Trove' were inscribed in Old English lettering.

Toby emerged with a stack of newspapers under his arm, and pointing across the road I said:

'Shall we go and buy ourselves a treasure?'

'Oh, haven't we got enough?' he grumbled. 'Oh, very well. I suppose one can always do with one more. Do mind these lorries, though. I don't believe they could stop, even if they wanted to.'

There was a hideous Victorian dining-table taking up half the space in the Trove showroom, with a ticket on it bearing the figure £120, among other meaningless symbols. It was piled with job lots of cutlery, wine glasses and dessert plates, but a space had been cleared at one end to make room for a battery of furniture-polishing equipment. Guy Robinson was seated there, on some library steps, shining a pair of shoes.

'We're closed,' he called out, in his merry Irish voice. 'But doan't let that be worrying yez. Come insoide, the both of yer, and cheer the auld fellah up.'

'You should hang a card out when you're closed,' I informed him. 'How is one supposed to know?'

'Well, the boss has taken off, d'ye see? Went out in the divil of a horry, and I can't seem to lay me hands on the blessed little card. Should never be surprised if she'd sold it, you know.'

'Will she be long?'

'Couldn't ever say, me darlin'. She's away to one of them auction sales, combin' the countryside for bargains.'

'In that case, we might do better to postpone our visit until she's combed it,' Toby suggested, glancing around.

'But you have masses of stuff here already,' I said firmly. 'And we don't exactly want to buy anything. Couldn't we just snoop around for a bit? How much is this lacquer tray?'

He told me and I put it down again, passing on to a Waterford jug, with a chip in the handle.

Toby remarked sociably that it made an interesting change to see someone cleaning shoes with furniture polish, since it was the custom in his house to use shoe polish on the furniture, and when he had recovered from his astonishment Guy told me that the reason for the Waterford jug being knocked down to twenty-five quid was that it had a chip in the handle, invisible to the naked oy. Then switching abruptly to his drawing-room comedy style he begged us to partake in a glass of sherry wine. He went across to an inlaid corner-cupboard, which also had a price tag dangling from its key, and took out a decanter and some glasses, saying:

'Or are you nervous about your tipples, after last night?'

'Not at all –'

'. . . Yes, very,' Toby and I replied in unison.

'Shocking business, isn't it?' Guy continued. 'Must have been suicide is the cry that goes up all around.'

He had turned his back on us and I noticed him put the decanter down and unobtrusively step aside to close the door between the shop and the back storeroom, which had been off the latch.

'What makes them cry any such thing?' I asked.

'Because, sweetie, the alternative is really too fantastic for sane men to contemplate, wouldn't you say? I mean, there we all were in the room with him when he died, and people don't up and murder one of the other guests in the middle of a party. At least, not in my experience.'

'And in mine they don't up and commit suicide, either.'

'I suppose it would depend on the party?' Toby suggested.

Guy gave a snort of laughter: 'Well, I admit the H.B.s do rather get away with murder – Oh, blimey, 'ark at 'im!

Now, don't get me wrong, folks. I was referring to those turgid movies they will keep inflicting on us.'

'As a matter of curiosity, had you seen that particular one before?'

'Know it by heart, darling. But, apart from that, they're very, very lovely people, as you must have seen. Xenia and I are devoted to them.'

'We may not have seen them at their best,' Toby admitted, 'and I really do think it's time we left, Tessa. I've got that soufflé on my mind. You can come back some other time and look for whatever it is you want.'

'Oh, but I do so love poking around, and another few minutes won't hurt. It always has to stand for an hour, before going in the oven. Haven't you got some more stuff in the back room, Guy?'

'Only a few oddments that haven't been priced yet. Pictures, mainly; and not for sale. The Russian eagle eye picked out one or two watercolours which might fetch a bit more than our average trade provides. We'll probably send them up to Sotheby's. How about this, now? Here's a pretty little troifle as'd suit a foine young lady like yeself.'

He was poised on tiptoe, leaning precariously forward over a mountain of assorted china, one arm reaching up to grasp a dusty Dresden mirror on the shelf above. Seizing my chance, I said quickly:

'Not now. Toby's right; we must dash. Good-bye and thanks awfully.'

'But you're leaving by the wrong door,' Toby pointed out.

'Oh, silly me, so I am!' I said, opening it, as I spoke.

I closed it again almost immediately, because Guy's reflexes were admirably tuned up and he had spun round and regained his balance in the space of seconds.

Nevertheless, my brief glimpse inside of the store-room had been enough to verify two guesses. One was that it contained a much larger collection of paintings than Guy had led us to believe; the other that it was no poltergeist who was responsible for the scuffling noises I had heard. For that brief instant, I had stared straight into the cringing, frightened eyes of Anabel Harper Barrington, who crouched on the floor, hugging her martyred old golden retriever.

Eight

(i)

'Did Guy realise you had seen her?' Robin asked, with mild interest, when I had poured an account of the foregoing events into his undeserving ear.

He had dashed into the house two minutes before lunch, looking *distrait* and self-important, and had incurred Aunt Moo's displeasure by wolfing down the soufflé as carelessly as though it were a baked apple, and mine by refusing to discuss the progress he was making with his darling friend, Superintendent Cole.

All he would say, and it was said without a smile, was that, owing to the fortuitous circumstance of his being on the spot, Scotland Yard had officially requested him to remain and give what assistance he could to the local branch in the little matter of Sir Maddox Brand's murder.

If he had expected his audience to swoon with excitement he must have been disappointed. Toby gave it as his opinion that policemen were not only getting younger, but the arm of their coincidence growing longer every day; and Aunt Moo's comment that poor Maddox had been a very curious man was made in such dismissive tones as to suggest that this provided the last word on the subject. To compensate, she assured us that he had not only been curious about pictures but other things as well.

My own retort took the form of congratulating her on the sacrifice of the Monday papers. The only mention of Sir Maddox's death, apart from the official obituary, was the faintly misleading statement that he had collapsed and died while dining with friends a few miles from his home. The moral of this, I pointed out, was that if anything sensational did occur on Sunday it stood little chance of being accurately reported on Monday.

It was irritating to find that, instead of deflating Robin, these reflections merely increased his complacency, and he said that this was where the trained eye could be an advantage. It often enabled its owner to see more than met the untrained one.

He unbent a little, when the other two had padded upstairs for their afternoon naps and we were alone together in the library, but only to tell me more about Old King Cole and how wonderful he was.

'Lived here all his life, you know,' he added proudly. 'His father was head gamekeeper to the people who owned the Court before Sir Maddox came, so he knows this part of the world like the back of his hand.'

'That's bound to come in useful,' I said. 'Seeing that the old boy was knocked off in what was virtually a padded cell.'

'I don't think we should let ourselves get too bogged down by that circumstance; but an intimate knowledge of the locality may turn out to be more valuable than you think.'

'You mean there might be some connection between this and the burglaries? Are you on to something? But that's terrific, Robin!'

'Now, for God's sake, don't jump to conclusions and then expect me to justify them. Naturally, it's always been on the cards that the two things were linked in some way, but we haven't got any closer to proving it. In any case, that's not what I had in mind. Where Cole is so useful is in supplying background information about all the people involved. It would take me months to complete the kind of unofficial dossiers he's collected on them. He's a great fan of your aunt's, by the way.'

'Who isn't?' I asked. 'At least, to be fair, I know of one who wasn't, but he hardly counts any more.'

'You mean Brand? Well, the odd thing is that Cole says they were thick as thieves until just lately.'

'Not literally, I hope,' I said, thinking of the cargoes of loot which Harbart was ferrying down to the Treasure Trove.

'But you must agree it's peculiar, in view of the unpleasant way he spoke about her to you?'

'Not necessarily. He was the type who would be as chummy as hell with someone when it suited him, and the next minute say the most slanderous things behind their backs.'

'I maintain that it was odd of him to pick on you to say them to; unless he intended you to repeat them.'

'Well, I didn't; and nor did she poison him off in a fit of pique, whatever darling old Cole may believe. For one thing, she was within two feet of me the whole time; and you know perfectly well that if she'd wanted to poison him she'd have got Dolly or Harbart to do it for her.'

'There you go again! Of course, Cole doesn't suspect her. It's simply that we're interested in every tiny anomaly that cropped up just before he died, and there happens to be a discrepancy here, which might be significant in some way.'

'Well, I can tell you of a tiny something or other which cropped up just after he died,' I said, 'although whether Superman Cole will attach any significance to it is another thing.'

It was then that I described our visit to the Treasure Trove, and of finding Anabel concealed there.

'I don't know whether Guy guessed I had seen her, or not,' I said, answering his question, 'but she knew it and, despite all that machinery in her mouth, she will no doubt manage to get the message through. In any case, it's not Guy's attitude which concerns me. He is exactly the sort of childish creature who would think it a great lark to give political asylum to a run-away adolescent. I should have thought the puzzling part was why she had run away at all, and why her mother, instead of informing the police and dragging the river, has simply taken to her bed and let the whole thing slide.'

'She's probably pattered off home, by now. In any case, we know she's safe, and we have far worse problems than Anabel confronting us.'

'Such as the little item the untrained eye missed in the newspaper this morning? I do think you might tell me what it was.'

He handed me the paper, folded into four, to show the bottom right-hand corner. Even so, it took me a minute or two to catch on, because the relevant item consisted of four lines of blotchy type in the Stop Press section. It announced that unidentified intruders had broken into Haverford Court during the early hours of Monday morning. Police were investigating, but nothing was thought to have been stolen.

'How extraordinary! What do you make of it?'

Robin shook his head: 'Nothing whatever, at present. All we know is exactly what you read there. It's just one more loose end.'

He would not discuss it further, saying that Cole expected him back for a meeting at three o'clock. So there was no opportunity to tell him of other small discoveries the Treasure Trove had yielded. Nor did I consider it necessary. If Cole was half the paragon Robin believed him to be, he would need no prompting from me to take a peep at all those pictures which were also shacked up in the Robinsons' store-room. He might even find, among the oddments of glass tucked away in their corner cupboard, the pair of tumblers which were identical to the one from which Sir Maddox had drunk his last vodkatini.

(ii)

After all, there was a miniature hue and cry over Anabel's flight, but it did not get to the pitch of dragging the river, or even of promoting a tussle in my own conscience. Before I was called upon to speak out, or forever hold my peace, she was back at home.

Dolly, the messenger of these tidings, told me that she had been bundled there in Mrs Zany's station-wagon, late on Monday evening; and I concluded that, having combed the countryside for bargains and not best pleased to find the space for them appropriated by a girl and her dog, she had lost no time in disposing of them.

It would have been a tame ending, indeed, to the escapade, although fitting enough for one involving Anabel, who seemed destined for a life of futile gestures; but, happily, one small mystery remained. The dog was still missing.

Dolly had rather a fanciful explanation for this, which was hardly surprising, since the account had come down to her from Maria, via Anabel, both of whom could be guaranteed to create confusion out of the simplest statement. The story went that, at some point during the afternoon, Anabel had let the dog into the Robinsons' back garden and, seeing it limp away on its own devices, had turned indoors again. Twenty minutes later, when she went back, it had vanished, and she had spent the remaining daylight hours combing the countryside for a golden retriever, punctuated by regular return visits to the Treasure Trove, but all to no avail.

There was something undeniably fishy about this tale, as a dog of that size and colour, with one game leg, was hardly in a position to cover much ground, nor to pass for long unobserved by the neighbours. However, neither Robin nor Toby considered the matter to be worthy of their attention, and I was left with one more unanswered question to add to my file.

The inquest was scheduled to take place in Lewes on Tuesday morning, but the Superintendent, ever vigilant in sparing me contact with harsh reality, had decreed that my presence would not be required. Unfortunately, I could neither use the time to pursue my personal investigations of the Harper Barrington's, nor to coerce Christabel into getting out the palette and making a start on my portrait, since all three of them had been summoned to give evidence.

Mooning about in the library, I came across a book of Daniel Mott reproductions and sat down at the desk, turning the pages slowly as I studied each in turn, and pausing even longer over those which featured Christabel. There was a set of four sketches of her, taking up the centre double page. She was depicted on a characteristically tousled bed, with her back half-turned to the artist, apparently scrutinising her toenails. In my philistine fashion, I found all the drawings fairly dull and anaemic, but had to concede that there was something about the curve of her back in one of them, which was a trifle heart-stopping. Having nothing better to do, I took a pencil and writing-pad and began to copy the sketch.

I cannot pretend that my efforts were remotely successful and Toby, who came alongside as I was adding some shady bits to the fourth attempt, fell about laughing.

'I'm improving,' I protested. 'All I need is a little more practice.'

'What you need is some tracing-paper,' he said, taking the pencil out of my hand and dashing off a few rapid strokes on one corner of the page.

'That's rather good,' I admitted sadly, as he twisted it round for me to see. 'Just as good as the original.'

'No, it's not; and the point is it's not original. It's just a flash trick. You might have acquired it, yourself, if you hadn't floated through the art class, dreaming of your name in lights in Shaftesbury Avenue.'

'But it's not in lights, there or anywhere else, and not likely to be, at the rate I'm going. Altogether, this has been a mortifying morning; everything conspiring to show up my own inadequacies. I've had about enough.'

'Don't despair,' he said consolingly. 'We must never forget that no effort, however fatuous, is totally wasted. In my experience, it can sometimes lead to no end of trouble.'

'I suppose that might be better than nothing,' I agreed.

NINE

(i)

IN DUE course we learnt that the jury, not quite on its toes in the opinion of some, had brought in an open verdict. Whereupon, Toby, ignoring my entreaties and having presumably received the green light from Mrs Parkes, slipped merrily away in a Mercedes spruced up as never before after two days of Harbart's tender care.

Thc throng of journalists, who had spent the previous twenty-four hours clamped to the gates of The Maltings and Haverford Court, gradually drifted away. By twelve o'clock the next morning, they had drifted back again, the news having broken that the barn had been burnt to a cinder, an event subsequently referred to as 'Murder Village Blaze', and Christabel was in hospital on the danger list.

Mercifully, both reports proved to be slightly exaggerated, but Robin told me that Christabel's injuries were serious enough to cause anxiety.

'Don't blame me,' he said defensively. 'I didn't set fire to her blessed old barn.'

'Well, who did?'

'How should I know? I should think the cause will be fairly easy to establish, but it's being investigated of course. In fact, they're crowding in on us from all sides. For one thing, it was scheduled as an historic building, so the preservation people are rattling their sabres. Also Mott's pictures were insured for a pretty hefty sum, so we've got the assessors round our necks, as well. They'll be dead keen to sniff out a bit of arson, if they can. Unfortunately, the flames had got such a hold by the time anyone thought of sending for the fire brigade they they're going to have their work cut out.'

'Who's anyone? Didn't Christabel give the alarm, herself?'

'No, it was someone from the Court, who happened to notice smoke; the gardener's wife, in fact. Christabel had no telephone, as you know, and she's more or less isolated. This gardener's cottage is the nearest human habitation, and it's seven or eight minutes' walk. It doesn't seem to have occurred to her to go there. Apparently, she was obsessed by saving as many pictures as she could and she simply pitched in and started dragging them out, by herself.'

'Poor old thing! What a lion she is! Did she manage to rescue many?'

'Quite a few. Then she must have been knocked out by the fumes. They found her lying across the threshold. She was lucky, because the whole doorway collapsed within minutes of their getting to her.'

'Can I see her?'

'Not for a day or two. She's not even strong enough to talk to us at present.'

'You said you knew how the fire was started. Was that true, or just a guess?'

'I prefer to call it a conclusion based on observation. I believe she started it herself. Oh, not deliberately, I don't mean that. But you know how careless she is, and always got a cigarette going? It's my belief that she dropped a lighted match or fag-end somewhere in the barn. It wouldn't have needed more than that. The old place was as dry as a tinder-box, and there was sawdust and bits of sacking to help things along. Some of the pictures were still packed in wooden crates.'

I shook my head: 'Sorry to knock such a nice, convenient theory, Robin, but it won't do. I know she's careless and slops around like a tramp and all that, but it's only because she's sacrificed everything, vanity included, to those old pictures. Her entire life revolves round them. Honestly, I do know what I'm talking about, and I'll bet you a million that she wouldn't have lit a match, or even smoked a cigarette inside the barn, any more than I would whistle in my dressing-room. It was ingrained.'

He looked impressed by this argument, but muttered something about Christabel getting a bit past it, and of elderly people often having mental lapses.

'Oh, come off it,' I said. 'You know jolly well that she isn't senile in that sense, and she's only three days more elderly than she was last Sunday.'

'What's that supposed to mean?'

'When Christabel told us that somebody had broken into the barn last Saturday night, you went over there to look round, didn't you? And did you find one single trace of a spent match, or cigarette ash scattered around, which would given you reason to think she might have been careless in that way?'

'No,' he admitted, frowning. 'No, I can't say I did.'

'There you are, then!'

'That's only negative evidence; it doesn't prove anything. Still, I'll grant you this much. Now you mention it, I do recall that, apart from some of the pictures having been recently tumbled around, the place was remarkably neat and tidy. There was no dust, and I remember thinking that, in a lot of ways, it was a damn sight better cared for than the cottage.'

He made this admission very soberly, and remained staring down at the table when he had finished speaking.

I said: 'All right! What else?'

'What else what?'

'You don't fool me; I know that face. What else have you remembered?'

'Well, if you must know, it's I who am getting senile. Talk about mental lapses! Thank God it was you who caught me out, and not the Assistant Commissioner. Do you know, until you brought it up, I'd forgotten all about that incident of the burglary on Saturday? I suppose it's because so many more pressing things have come up since then, but it's inexcusable and I'm grateful to you for reminding me.'

'It was not a thing I was likely to forget. I feel sure it has an important place in the scheme of things.'

He was not listening: 'There has to be a connection, I suppose,' he went on, pursuing his own train of thought, 'though for the life of me I can't see how it ties in. Could we be looking at it from the wrong angle? I mean, supposing it wasn't a burglary at all, but an abortive attempt to set fire to the barn? That would account for nothing being stolen.'

'I think something was stolen, but go on.'

'Well, say that Christabel was alerted before this intruder was able to get to work with the paraffin or whatever, last Saturday? Why shouldn't he have come back a day or two later and had a second shot?'

'Yes, that makes sense.'

'I honestly think it does, Tessa. Much more sense than the other way round. God knows who would want to do such a thing, or why; but at least it gives us one individual to deal with, instead of two separate ones.'

'I think that's a brilliant deduction,' I said. 'Good for you!'

I meant it, too. The only snag was that, if his version was correct, it drove a couple of bulldozers through my own personal theories concerning the purpose and identity of Christabel's Saturday-night intruder.

So, as soon as he had left for his afternoon session with darling old Cole, I retired to my room to review the situation in this new light and to see how best to trim and rearrange two irreconcilable theories and fuse them into one coherent whole.

*

(ii)

The answer was not long in coming, though any tendency to complacency on that score was soon offset by the chastening reflection that a personal inspection of the barn must now be placed first on my agenda.

This, decidedly, was not an expedition to be undertaken impulsively, since Robin had warned me that assessors, investigators and preservers were thick on the ground. Nevertheless, I doubted if much assessing or preserving would be carried out after six o'clock in the evening and, in these late August days, there was still daylight until about nine. Dinner at The Towers was at eight sharp, but Robin had fallen into the habit of foregoing this, in favour of Superintendent Cole's country custom of an early cold spread at the pub. Taking all these factors into account, I selected seven o'clock for my witching hour.

However, there were various preliminary stages to be gone through first, and no amount of straining at the leash could make their performance possible until the following day. I therefore resigned myself to another evening of Beggar My Neighbour, followed by the kind of television game, so dear to the heart of Aunt Moo, where the contestants get a big hand for saying that Paris is the capital of France, and bring the roof down if they admit to being old-age pensioners.

(iii)

My plan did not appear half so enticing in the cold light of Thursday morning, but the prospect of another languid day stretching interminably ahead, without even Toby to lighten it, was enough to gird the loins; and soon after ten I set forth on the first stage of my programme, which was a call at the local hospital.

As I had foreseen, Christabel was still unfit to receive visitors, so I handed over the fruit and flowers which I had gathered on the way, plus a cold grouse, thoughtfully provided by Aunt Moo. The white-haired, white-coated lady at the reception desk was not pleased. She told me that she could not say, she was sure, who would find the time to take them up to Miss Blake, and they were already just about snowed under. She drew my attention to a harvest-festival display, piled up on one end of her counter, saying bitterly:

'Some people seem to think that's what we're here for. Running about after vases. I'll do my best for you, of course, but we don't get time to breathe in this place.'

'You mean all that lot is for Miss Blake, too? I had no idea she was such a popular figure.'

'Oh, they've been arriving all morning; Interflora, telephone calls, the lot. People must have seen it in the papers, I suppose, What would she be, then? Some kind of a celebrity?'

'In her way,' I replied absently, squinting inquisitively at some of the cards on these floral tributes. Most were discreetly concealed in their tiny envelopes, but an elegant gold hamper, containing hothouse grapes, boxes of sweets and jars of peaches in brandy, tastefully draped round a familiar-looking bottle of champagne, bore an ordinary visiting-card, well to the fore.

'Here's one that doesn't need vases, at any rate,' I said.

'Oh yes, Mrs H.B. She's got more sense. But then, she knows what we're up against.'

I would have dearly liked to delve a little deeper into this cryptic statement, but people were pressing up behind me, breathing anxiously down my neck; and, besides, there was a danger of getting behind in my schedule.

A green double-decker bus with HAVERFORD across its forehead was standing in the village square, which was just as it should have been, if the timetable were anything to go by, and I hurtled aboard and clambered up on top just as it moved off.

From my seat over the driver's head, I had a front-row, dress-circle view of the terrain and I could see the bridle track, leading to Mill Cottage, wiggling off at right-angles to the road minutes before we reached it. It was evidently not a popular stop, for the conductor clanged his bell and we sailed past, without even slowing down. I checked my watch and found that, so far, the journey had taken exactly twelve minutes.

The police station was only a few hundred yards from Haverford Market Place, which was the bus terminal, but when I entered it the sergeant in charge told me that Robin was not available. 'Tied up' was the expression he used, and in many ways I felt it to be a fitting one.

I announced my identity and explained that I had been hoping to get a lift back to Burleigh. Whereupon, he became all smiles, saying that Robin was out somewhere with the Super, and fractionally anticipating my request to take the weight off my feet in his office. There can be few human beings for whom a sergeant in that position feels more warmly than the lone female who wanders apologetically up to his desk, and then turns out not to have lost her dog, her purse or her memory.

The Superintendent's office was an austere, cell-like kind of room, with one high window giving on to a dirty brick wall. There were no confidential files on the desk to take a peep at, not even a photograph of Mrs Cole or an engagement diary to provide diversion. I found some inter-office memo-sheets and scrawled a note, with a funny drawing on it, for Robin; then fooled around for a bit with some rubber stamps. But I had to tuck the results of this rather hastily into my bag, for there was a tap on the door and my sergeant friend stuck his head round to ask if I fancied a cup of tea. I told him I had changed my mind about waiting for Robin, because there was a bus leaving for Burleigh in a few minutes and, if I hurried, I could just catch it.

In the event, it left without me because, as I passed the Bank, Xenia came stamping out, carrying a battered and swollen green satchel, and offered me a lift in the station-wagon.

I would gladly have refused, having labelled her an eccentric type and most probably a foul driver, but as I had begun by announcing that I was hurrying for the bus there was no backing out.

True to my worst fears, she drove with the fury of one holding the reins of a droshky, rather than a steering-wheel, with the pursuing wolf-pack actually sniffing at the rear bumper. Furthermore, she had not yet acquired the native custom, at least when negotiating hairpin bends, of driving on the left.

The ordeal was made even more intolerable by the fact that she had plonked the bulging satchel on the passenger seat and had commanded me to sit in the back. I disliked this intensely, both because it put me out of reach of the controls and because there was a smelly old rug covering the back seat, impregnated with dust and orange hairs. To achieve the minimum contact with it, I perched on the extreme edge, leaning forward over the seat in front and mentally measuring the distance between myself and the handbrake.

'You've got a pile of loot there,' I said, prodding the satchel, as a surreptitious means of giving my arm a trial run, in preparation for emergencies.

'No, no; just the paying-in books and some change for the till,' she said, barely resisting, I could see, the impulse to slap my hand away.

'Oh, do you have a till? How funny, I never noticed. I called at your shop the other day. Did Guy tell you?'

'The till is in the back room. We have to keep accounts and this makes it not so complicated.'

'Yes, it must do. Did Guy tell you I was there?'

'Guy tells me everything,' she said flatly.

'I don't see how you can be so positive. In my case, for instance, I know what Robin does tell me, though I often forget it again; but how could I know what he hadn't told me? Anabel was there, too, when I called. Did Guy tell you that?'

'You are a funny girl,' Xenia said, not laughing.

'Yes, I know, but did he tell you about Anabel and her dog being there when I called?'

'Oh, that Anabel! She is a bit soft. She is unhappy with her mother sometimes.'

'Well, there's nothing specially soft about that. I am sure Nancy is a very nice, efficient woman, but it's quite normal to hate your mother, at that age. At least, perhaps not in Russia, but in all the Western democracies it's quite the accepted thing. Something to do with sexual jealousy, I believe; father fixations and all that jazz.'

'Ah ça, alors! That jealousy is on another foot.'

'Is it? Whose foot? I wonder why all these cars keep flashing their headlights at us?'

'I do not know,' she said simply, proving that she was occasionally capable of giving a straight answer to a plain question.

'Well, I wish they'd stop; it makes me nervous. Whose foot is the jealousy on?'

'I am saying nothing. Anabel is no affair of mine.'

'I suppose not, but perhaps she is rather fond of you; of you both, I mean. So that when she runs away from the hated mother she shacks up with you?'

'Oh, she gives me some help in her holidays. Washing the china and this sort of thing. There is too much work in a place like that. These are your gates, I think,' she added, standing on the foot brake with such violence that I began to see the wisdom of relegating passengers to the back seat. They looked like the pearly gates to me, and I had never before found such comfort in the sight of Aunt Moo's four silly turrets.

I stumbled out and turned to thank Xenia for the lift, but before I could speak she made what was for her an unusually straightforward observation:

'You ask too many questions,' she said. 'You have not been well brought up.'

This, on top of the nerve-racking drive, left me utterly bereft, and I tottered up the drive, composing at least three splendid but wasted retorts between the gate and the front door.

Robin returned only ten minutes afterwards, so I could have spared myself all the dicing with death; but, as Toby had reminded me, no effort is ever wholly wasted and I believed I had advanced one, or maybe even one and a half steps along the way to tracking down my quarry.

Ten

'Who inherits?' I asked.

'A wife and two grown-up sons; both married and far away,' Robin replied, an ability to mind-read having been thrown in, along with all the other qualities. 'Two are abroad, and the third lives in Yorkshire.'

'And all properly accounted for?'

'Yes, no chance of Nancy or Xenia turning out to be the missing heiress. Isn't that a shame?'

'What about this wife, though? It's the first I've heard of one.'

'Well, she's number two, and they parted some years ago. The mother of the two boys divorced him and subsequently remarried, so she's out. Wife number two just seems to have drifted away. There was no legal separation, though, and apart from one major bequest the bulk of the estate is divided between these three.'

'What major bequest?'

'He left his art collection to the nation.'

'You don't say? Do you suppose he had informed the Prime Minister of the fact and that's what got him the knighthood?'

'Most likely.'

'Does it alter the situation? I mean, the thieves have now got some of the taxpayers' property on their hands.'

'I should think the chances are that's off their hands again by now. And don't I wish I knew where? In any case, only stuff from his London flat was stolen. Most of the collection was kept down here, so the nation will be doing all right for itself. So will the other beneficiaries, incidentally, and thereby hangs a tale.'

'Does it? I thought you said that distance lent enchantment to their alibis?'

'Not that kind of tale. This is something that happened years ago, and it concerns the wife. You remember my saying I thought I had seen Brand somewhere before?'

'Yes, I do.'

'Well, I had, but it was in a different context. He was plain Mr Brand then. Must have been before he made the will. I was a humble sergeant in Dedley in those days; long before you came into my life.'

'And changed all that. Do go on. She wasn't mixed up in a sensational art-theft, by any chance?'

'No, although I do remember that the house was crammed with valuables. It was about ten miles north of Dedley and we had to go there one fine day to interview the family about a suicide.'

'Oh, really? More cyanide in the vodka?'

'No, this was a hanging job. Suicide, without a doubt, but it was a specially nasty case, because the victim was a schoolgirl. Fifteen or so. She was the niece of the second Mrs Brand and she spent most of her school holidays with her.'

'Orphan?'

'No; family split up. There was an older child, in the custody of the father, and this one got planted on her mother, who doesn't seem to have had much time for her.'

'That has a familiar ring. Not a thing to bring on suicide, though?'

'She didn't leave a note or anything, but the motive was pretty obvious. She was three months gone, which I suppose was a little more cogent ten or twelve years ago than it would be today.'

'I can see it being fairly cogent, even today, if one were fifteen and in the clutches of that wicked step-uncle. I take it he was the father of this embryo?'

'Well, as I say, she didn't leave a note. At least, if she did, someone saw fit to destroy it before we arrived on the scene; but it was fairly clear that Mrs Brand believed her old man was responsible, even though nothing would have made her admit it. She went abroad soon afterwards, which

I suppose is about as positive an indictment as one would be likely to get. He never altered his will, curiously enough, so perhaps he always hoped she would come back.'

'Or he may simply have believed he was immortal.'

'No, it wasn't that, because he took the trouble to add a codicil only six months ago. Anyway, the pay-off is that soon after his wife left Brand sold the house and moved down here. Now read on.'

'Oh, I will; and, if you ask me, it's: Chapter Two – Anabel. Only there's a new twist now. We might call it The Hangman Hanged.'

'You're still riding that hobby-horse, are you? I must admit that this other girl's suicide lends colour to your wild allegations; but I have to warn you that you're on shaky ground if you believe that he was killed because he was trying to seduce Anabel, or had already done so. We've interviewed both the Harper Barringtons until the cows came home and there's not a wisp of evidence that either of them regarded Brand as anything but a jolly, harmless old uncle, so far as Anabel was concerned.'

'If they thought otherwise, I dare say you would not be the one they would confide in.'

'I know, but there are tricks to make people betray themselves, often without their knowing they've done so, and I promise you that this is the blindest alley you've ever trod. The truth is, Tessa, Roger is not her real father. That's for your ears alone and, for God's sake, don't pass it on. And I can't tell you any more than that because I got my information in the strictest confidence. I just wanted you to know why I haven't much faith in your paternal-vengeance theory.'

'Who is her father, then?'

'I've told you; my lips are sealed. Sorry!'

The big trouble with men, it often seems to me is that their principles are either inviolate, or non-existent. They seem unable to strike a balance. However, when he used this tone, I knew there was nothing to be gained by pressing him and that it behoved me, rather, to be thankful he had divulged so much. Indeed, the return to something approaching his normal expansiveness had made me wonder once or twice during the narrative whether all was quite as merry as it had been at the Court of Old King Cole.

Sure enough, just as he was leaving, he remarked that he was growing a little tired of his six-thirty cheese-and-pickles routine and felt inclined to pass it up for once in favour of one of Aunt Moo's dinners.

This did not suit my book at all and I sternly reminded him that anything less than twenty-four hours' notice would make the pot so unbelievably chancy, by Aunt Moo's standards, that she would moan about it for a week.

He appeared to accept this unquestioningly, though grinning at me as he turned to go and saying:

'Yes, it must be dreadful for you having to be on time for meals and so forth. The wear and tear of it even seems to have dimmed your normal feverish curiosity.'

'Now, what do you mean by that? Don't go, Robin.'

'I must. Cole will be tapping his feet. But I notice you omitted to ask me about that tiny codicil, and who gets what.'

'Very well. Who gets what?'

'Anabel,' he replied. 'One thousand pounds. In trust till she's eighteen.'

Eleven

(i)

It was as well that Robin was so ignorant of Aunt Moo's true nature as to believe anything I might care to dish out on the subject, because, in fact, nothing gave her a bigger thrill than a young man's hearty appetite, and one of her principal squawks was that Robin was so rarely present at mealtimes.

I had already brought wrath on my own head by announcing that I should be out to dinner and by remaining adamant in this decision even when she had outlined the menu. I explained that there was a flick on in Haverford, which made even a sacrifice on this scale worth while, so stunning and sensational was it reputed to be.

I think it may have been true, too, because the Haverford bus was packed to the roof when I boarded it for the second time that day, and I scrambled into the last empty seat on the lower deck.

I was the only passenger to alight at the bridle path and I plodded along with not a soul in sight, remembering the last time I had passed that way, filled with airy dreams about my new quiet personality. Circumstances had obliged me to abandon that rôle before I had even worked myself into it, but I had dressed in the appropriate style for this occasion, too; and for a reason which was equally romantic, in its way. It is always easier to build up a characterisation, when the trappings are authentic and, having now transformed myself into the cat-burglar rôle, about to make surreptitious and agile flits round a shabby old brown ruin, had put on shabby old brown trousers and pullover, the better to melt into the background, not forgetting a shabby old brown satchel bag in which to stash away the loot.

I had been tempted to wear plimsolls, as well, to add the finishing touch *par excellence* but had been deterred by the thought that Aunt Moo might find them altogether too unsuitable for cinema-going, and after all I was glad of it. The bridle track was rough and stony and the half-mile trudge brought discomfort enough, without extra burdens. Furthermore, it soon became clear that the rest of the carefully-thought-out costume was no more than a token to art, since any agile flitting I was able to conduct would have to be carried out with the full knowledge and consent of the law.

A police constable was stationed outside what had once been the main entrance to the barn. His bicycle was propped against a nearby tree and he was seated on the grass, with his helmet beside him. When he noticed my approach, he pretended to have taken it off to scratch his head, and hurriedly replacing it, clambered to his feet.

'Good evening, Miss.'

'Good evening, Officer.'

'Sorry, Miss; no one allowed inside,' he said sternly, as I continued my inexorable advance.

Naturally, I had expected this, and I said: 'Oh, but Officer, darling, I only want to go in just for one tiny minute. My husband is Detective Inspector Price, you know, and he was sure it would be all right. I promise not to do any harm, but I'm a friend of Miss Blake and she has specially asked me to check on the state of one or two of her valuable pictures. She can't ask one of you, because you might not understand which ones she meant. As you know, she's very seriously ill and I'm terribly afraid all this worry is going to make her worse, unless I can put her mind at rest.'

It had been a forlorn hope all along, and, although he claimed to sympathise profoundly, my heart-rending appeal had not shaken him by so much as a tremor.

'Very sorry, Madam. I'd be glad to help you, but there's no one allowed in there without a permit. Those are my orders.'

'Oh, of course,' I said gaily, digging around in the enormous bag for my second and more chancy round of ammunition, and trusting it not to blow up in my face. 'Of course, I have a permit. Fancy forgetting that! I should have shown it to you at once, shouldn't I? There we are! Does that make everything all right?'

He studied the form for rather longer than it was strictly convenient to hold my breath; but, even to my eyes, the rubber stamp had done an impressive job, and I had gambled on his not detecting a forgery in the squiggled initials. After staring at it for what seemed about ten minutes, he folded it carefully and put it away in his pocket, saying:

'Well, that seems to be in order, Madam, so I cannot obstruct your entry, but I must warn you that this here barn is in a highly unsafe condition.'

'And I'll be most terribly careful, I promise you. What I have to do will only take a few minutes. Oh, thanks most awfully.'

'Just a minute, Madam,' he called, as I shot towards the gaping doorway. 'Just one thing. How long do you really expect it to take you?'

This was an unforeseen hitch, but I tried to sound nonchalant:

'Oh, not more than ten minutes. Well, fifteen at the outside.'

He removed his helmet again and this time he really did scratch his head, regarding me doubtfully:

'It's just that, well, if you could see your way to stopping on a bit longer, say twenty minutes, I might just pop over and have a bit of a chat with my sister, just to break the monotony, like. It's not far. She's married to the gardener up at the Court, and that's their cottage over there, other side of the trees.'

'Oh, sure! Go ahead,' I said effusively. 'Take your time. I'm in no hurry and I'll keep an eye on everything till you get back.'

I was practically jigging about with joy and amazement, my single regret being that I could never tell Robin about the lax and sloppy attitudes prevailing in the lower echelons of the Superintendent's staff. No such eventuality had apparently occurred to this simple-minded constable either, for he said, 'Ta very much, then', jumped on his bicycle and whizzed off.

I reckoned that the journey would take him four or five minutes in each direction, giving me a minimum of twenty to accomplish my business. This was twice as much as I had hoped for and enabled me to approach the task in a much more scientific fashion than the hit-and-miss method I had envisaged.

It was depressing to see the barn, which had once been a noble building, all of a hundred feet long and fifty wide, in such a desolate state. Most of the solid oak rafters and crossbeams were now mere blackened skeletons, all but one section of the roof had fallen in, and its charred, crumbling tiles littered the ground inside and out. There was a dirty, acrid smell and the cement floor was ankle-deep in water.

Three-quarters of the building was in ruins and I almost despaired of picking my way through the rubble, far less of finding anything recognisable among the debris. Unfortunately, it must have been in the most badly affected part that Christabel had stored the bulk of her pictures, for I could see the skeletal remains of wooden crates and blackened frames strewn among the wreckage. However, there was one small section, over by the stable door, which had escaped the worst of the damage, and I picked my way cautiously towards it. It comprised only a small part of the whole, not more than twelve feet square, and there was a rope fencing it off from the rest, for what purpose I was at first unable to fathom, although the point was soon brought home to me in a disagreeable fashion.

I ducked under the rope and even this slight movement must have set up vibrations of some kind, for immediately great dollops of broken tiles came clattering down and landed only a foot away. I stopped dead, waiting with fascinated apprehension for the shower to cease and, when it had done so, edged slowly forward again, having measured the distance to the end wall, which was still intact, and keeping my eyes firmly fixed on the sagging roof.

I got across without further alarms, but what I had taken to be a pot of gold at the end of the trail turned out to be only half a dozen pictures, stacked in a single row against the wall. Although untouched by the fire, they were mostly too saturated with water to be any use, but there were two which had survived the worst of the hosing and which seemed worthy of inspection.

I squatted down and studied each in turn for several minutes, then pulled out one of Dolly's kitchen knives, which I had secreted in the bag, and carefully cut one of the canvases out of its damp frame. I was about to repeat the process with the second picture, when a sound from the other end of the barn caused me to drop the knife and twist round in a spasm of alarm.

I was in shadow at my end, whereas the other was streaked with patches of evening sunlight and I could distinguish little of the figure who stood, apparently watching me, just inside the entrance. I concluded it was the constable, returning ahead of schedule, and stood up, with an innocent expression on my face and black curses in my heart for sisters who were either away from home, or totally deficient in small talk.

However, as it advanced stealthily towards me, I saw that it was not the constable at all, but some ghastly mummified creature from outer space, and I let out a wild scream of terror.

A moment later, recovering myself and reverting to normal dialogue, I said:

'What are you doing here, for Christ's sake?'

'A good question. I was about to ask it.'

'But you're supposed to be on the danger list. How did you break out?'

'I have my methods,' she replied. 'Which I don't propose to go into now, because you haven't answered the question.'

'Oh, I was just passing,' I said vaguely, 'and I thought I'd take a look round. Sad to see the old place in this state, isn't it?'

'Very.'

'Yes, it is; very. And I apologise for screaming at you, Christabel, but I wasn't expecting anyone and you look so awful, bandaged up like that. I suppose I'm rather sensitive. How on earth did you get here?'

'By taxi. There's a rank right outside the hospital and the drivers are quite accustomed to corpses.'

I could hear her plainly, for her voice was growing more distinct all the time, but she had melted into the shadows again.

'Well, I'm not,' I said, 'and I'm sure you ought not to be out of bed. Where are you? Christabel!'

'Not far off. There is something I came to check on. It won't take me long.'

I, too, had been inching forward during this uneasy dialogue and suddenly she came into view again, only two feet beyond the dividing rope.

'What have you got in that bag, Tessa?'

I looked down at it, searching for the soft answer to turn away wrath:

'Nothing much. Compact . . . love letters . . . all that junk.'

'Look out!' she called sharply, and a reflex action sent my head jerking upwards and my eyes automatically to the roof. Unfortunately, these vaunted reflexes are not always such a safeguard as they are cracked up to be and the danger, whatever it was, must have come from another direction. Before I could locate, far less avert, it a stinging blow on the back of my head sent me reeling forward, to sprawl, first on my knees, and then face forward like a sack of potatoes, on to the concrete floor.

(ii)

Several years later, I opened my eyes, felt the grass beneath my raging head and saw Robin bending over me, looking almost as wan as I felt.

He said: 'You'll be the death of me one of these days. I'm telling you.'

'I'll be the death of myself first,' I replied, giggling inanely at what, in my feeble state, I considered to be a very witty riposte. 'How long have I been out?'

'About twenty minutes, I gather. How do you feel?'

'Terrible.'

'Well, lie still. Don't attempt to move. There's an ambulance on its way.'

'How did you get here so quickly? It's just like the Perils of Pauline.'

'Yes, isn't it? And the day you stop treating life as one long movie melodrama will be a bright one for all of us.'

My head ached and I was tired of inventing ripostes, witty or otherwise, so I closed my eyes and pretended to go unconscious again. This was quite a good riposte, too, in its way, for he instantly became all solicitude and very contrite, I could tell, for the burst of irritability.

'What hit me?' I inquired, cutting through the flow of anxious inquiry.

'Oh, you're still alive, are you? That's good! About a ton of falling masonry, by the look of it. Lie still now, and try to relax. I'll tell you about it later.'

'Tell me now,' I said, 'and I'll relax later.'

'I don't know the details yet, because he'd unburied you by the time I arrived, but all I can say is that it's a wonder you're here at all. Anyone else would have been blasted into oblivion.'

'We Paulines are made of sterner stuff,' I reminded him.

'And what that old fool, Christabel, thought she was up to beats me entirely. Anyway, she's another of the same breed, because she had to be dug out, too. Although, from what he told me, she must have had just enough warning to escape the worst of it.'

'Well, that's a relief. Who's this "he" you keep on about?'

'P.C. Jenner, who was on duty here this evening.'

'Oh, he came back, did he? What happened to the sister?'

'What sister?'

'I don't know, Robin. Some sister. I've forgotten which one. I'm terribly sorry.'

'Oh, don't worry; it's not a thing to worry about. She'll turn up, right as rain, you bet!' Robin said, with the forced cheerfulness of a nanny, temporarily out of her depth. 'Just lie still and we'll soon have you out of here. If only that damned ambulance would get a bloody move on!' he added, in less nannyish tones.

'Tell me more about old P.C. Thing, while we're waiting, Robin. He was quick off the mark, was he?'

'Jenner? Yes, a live wire, if ever I saw one.'

'If he's the one I met, it's my duty to tell you that this live wire has feet of clay.'

'On the contrary, he has the feet of Mercury and the brain of Socrates.'

I started to shake my head, thought better of it and said, with great deliberation: 'You have been sorrowfully misled, and I am very sorry.'

'My darling girl, the last thing I intend to do, in your present state, is to argue, but you shouldn't get these fixations about people. The fact is, it's entirely due to Jenner that you are more or less in one piece. There wasn't a chance of Christabel being able to dig you out single-handed, before you suffocated. It was quite tricky, even for a hale and hearty young man, and it was only the fact that he'd already rung us at the pub, too, for which I award extra marks, that won the day.'

'No, Robin, that can't be right. How could he telephone you, when there isn't one?'

'Not here, from the cottage; but, of course, you don't know about that, do you. You see, dove, he guessed there was something fishy about you, but since your permit appeared to be in order he could hardly bar your way. So he nipped over to the gardener's cottage, to check with Cole and me. By the time he got back, with instructions to put you in irons, half the barn was on top of you. But, as I say, he'd almost got you clear, by the time we arrived.'

'You mean that bit about his sister was just a yarn?'

'I'm not sure which sister you're referring to, or how she got into the act, but never mind that now. Here's the ambulance at last, I do declare.'

'I don't need an ambulance,' I protested. 'If you've got your car here, I can manage perfectly well.'

'Well, I haven't. Cole has taken it, to drive Christabel back to the hospital. He was all for our taking you, as well, but I wasn't risking having you bumped over all those potholes. Furthermore, you're going straight to the hospital yourself. I don't think that tough little skull is fractured, but we won't take any chances till it's been X-rayed. Now, keep perfectly still while they put you on the stretcher. The trick is to leave everything to them.'

I did as he told me, but just as the two ambulance attendants were loading me aboard I let out a scream of alarm which paralysed them with terror and left me suspended upright, feeling like a papoose whose mother had suddenly lost interest.

'My bag, Robin!' I yelled. 'I can't go without my bag. The big brown one.'

'What? Oh, was that yours? I didn't recognise it. Never mind, you don't need your mascara now, and it's quite safe. We thought it belonged to Christabel and it went in the car with her.'

(iii)

I was allotted a neat little cell, just off one of the main wards, and whiled away the time before my X-ray by supplying a sympathetic Irishwoman with my full name, date of birth and next of kin. After which, we dwelt at more length on the subject of her pet movie-star, in one of whose fillums I had played a small part. However, being an avid fan, she knew far more about him than I did, including oddly enough, his full name, date of birth and next of kin.

During the second interval, the radiologist reported that my skull was relatively undamaged; but, due maybe to my tiresome obsession with the missing bag, prescribed twenty-four hours' complete rest, with no over-excitement. This sounded to me like a perfect description of the average day at The Towers, but with the doctor's connivance Robin arranged for me to spend this period in hospital.

He did not tell me of the arrangement until it had been accomplished and, in answer to my protests, pointed out that hectic sessions of Beggar My Neighbour would certainly be classed, in medical circles, as over-excitement in a big way. On the other hand, if I were to be treated as an invalid, it would put a lot of extra work on poor old Dolly.

I weighed up these two alternatives and was bound to confess that neither was half so enticing as another cosy session with darling Nurse O'Malley, adding:

'In any case, I certainly don't intend to leave this place until they give me back my bag.'

'Oh, not that old bag again! What do you expect me to do about it? Tear the place apart with my bare hands?'

'Yes,' I said, 'I do.'

A few minutes later he returned and threw the bag down on my bed.

'There you are! All that carry on, and it was just as I said. They found it in Christabel's locker. Well? What now?'

'What now what?'

'Aren't you going to look inside and make sure it's all there?'

'No, not yet. I may do that later, but we've both had enough over-excitement to be going on with. I expect your own temperature might start soaring, if you had to chase round the hospital looking for the missing lipstick.'

'Too right, and it's getting late, so I'll leave you now, and you must try to sleep. I expect they'll give you a pill, so mind you take it. I'll look in first thing in the morning and see how you are. It's a relief to know that you can't get into mischief, at least for the next twelve hours.'

He was right, too, although my blameless night was not for want of trying. I made two determined sorties toward Christabel's room, once during the night and again in the early hours of the morning; but the door of that particular stable had been firmly shut, and on each occasion I found a policewoman camped outside it. Whether she was there to keep intruders out, or to keep Christabel in, I could not tell, but her expression was so forbidding that I sailed past, pretending to be on my way to the bathroom.

Probably there was nothing lost either, for it is doubtful if the room would have yielded any clue to the whereabouts of the rolled-up canvas. It was even less likely that Christabel would have handed it over on demand, having first gone to the trouble of removing it from my bag.

TWELVE

(i)

MY FIRST visitor of the day was Nancy Harper Barrington, who made a dramatic entrance soon after nine o'clock, having first flung wide the door and then bashed and bumped a double-decker, rubber-wheeled trolley into my room.

Having instantly worked myself into the belief that this heralded an imminent brain-operation, which no one had seen fit to tell me about, I fell back against the pillows again, quite faint with relief to discover that the top half contained nothing more alarming than a selection of the morning newspapers and some seedy-looking paperbacks. The lower shelf was stacked with cigarettes and confectionery.

The Lady Bountiful, herself, although pale, was evidently at peace with the world again, every hair in its correct position in the chignon, and looking very brisk and efficient in her natty white overall.

'Well, my dear, how are you?' she asked. 'I was on my rounds and I thought I'd look in for a sec.'

'How kind! I feel a little –'

'Well, that's good, my dear. I mustn't stop because I've got two miles of wards to get round, and one hell of a day in front of me.'

'Do you do this chore every morning.'

'No, only once or twice a month. We have a rota system and about twenty of us take it in turns. It's a frightful bind, but one feels one should do what one can.'

'And it must be pretty laborious, just getting that cumbersome great thing in and out. They ought to give you a small trolley, or else knock down some of the walls.'

'To be terribly candid, my dear, I'm not strictly supposed to go into the private rooms. So don't let on, will you? One is only meant to push it round the wards. Shattering bore, of course, but it cheers them up. Anyway, I thought I'd just take a peep and see how you were feeling.'

'That was sweet of you. I'm really not too bad now. Just a bit woolly, but . . .'

'Oh, I'm so glad. And, quite honestly, my dear, I envy you being waited on hand and foot and not a thing to worry about, I literally do. Tell me what happened, though. I'm dying to hear.'

Naturally, I had prepared an answer for this one, having composed a little tale in anticipation of the question coming up fairly frequently in the next few days. Unfortunately, I did not get much chance to practice it on Nancy.

'The snag is, I can't remember very clearly,' I began. 'It's still rather blurred. . . .'

'I suppose you've heard Dolores has walked out on me?' she interrupted.

'No, I hadn't. When?'

'Day before yesterday. Just up and left, without a word. No notice, nothing! Isn't it too positively sickening?'

'And no explanation?'

'Well, you know what these peasants are, my dear! Utterly superstitious about death and so on. She was a very tiresome girl, in many ways, though I simply can't think how I shall manage without her. The Maltings is only a tiny little place, as you know, but it's out of the question to try and run it without at least two servants, specially in the holidays. Jeremy will be arriving home from Yorkshire at any moment, with literally trunkloads of dirty clothes.'

'Yorkshire? I thought he was staying with the King of Northumbria?'

'Oh well, same thing. The point is, my dear, that if I don't get somebody soon I shall be spending my entire life bending over the washing-machine.'

'I hope it won't come to that. What about a temporary?'

'I'd rather not. Most of them are so careless and irresponsible. Dolores was bad enough and one wouldn't want one's few remaining treasures to be smashed to smithereens. As a matter of fact, I was hoping to get round Mrs Hankinson to lend me Dolly for an hour or two every morning. If you're going back there today, do put in a word for me, will you?'

It was my private conviction that nothing less than a word from the Almighty would have engineered such a sacrifice and, shirking the issue, I said:

'But you still have Maria. Can't she rustle up a cousin or something?'

'Oh, my faithful old Maria! She's been with us for years. Honest as the day and utterly devoted; but, to be perfectly frank with you, my dear, I'm not too keen to take a recommendation from her. It was Maria who foisted Dolores on me, and she's been nothing but a nuisance since the day she arrived.'

From the serious way in which she related all this, it was apparent that Nancy believed that no subject on earth could hold a greater fascination for me; but I am not easily swept off my feet by other people's domestic tribulations. Moreover, even twelve hours in hospital was long enough to inflict one symptom which is common to most inmates, namely a profound detachment from the hurly-burly of life outside those cloistered walls, combined with an equally profound ennui towards visitors whose range of conversation did not restrict itself principally to the patient's condition.

I endeavoured to smother my yawns and not allow my eyes to slide too often towards the book I had been reading before she came in, and I must have succeeded pretty well in concealing my indifference, for she sat on, gassing away interminably about employment agencies and temporary cooks, until Nurse O'Malley broke it up by entering as one pursued by a bear as she whisked a thermometer out of her starched bib.

When she had helped Nancy to reverse the trolley out into the corridor, she perched herself on the window ledge, saying:

'She's a good sort, that Mrs H.B. Really and truly. Just a bit nosey, that's all it is. Still, she'd be a friend of yours, I dare say?'

I still had my jaws clamped on the thermometer, so the only way to deny it was to waggle my head and hum.

'Oh, my hat, you can take it out now. Must have been in good two minutes, wouldn't you say? And let's hope you're nice and normal. Yes, you are! You're a good girl, you know. And she means well, I don't doubt. She has a gorgeous house, so they tell me.'

'It's not bad,' I said. 'Not what I'd choose, but not bad. I could tell you a fascinating thing about that house, though, O'Malley, darling.'

'Could you now? And what would that be?'

'It's becoming a very popular place for running away from.'

(ii)

Dolly was the next to arrive. She staggered in, loaded with half a ton of groceries, and told me I was looking peaky, before moving on to the even less welcome news that Robin had been summoned to a conference in London and would not be back until the evening.

'And he says you're to stay right where you are, dear, and not to dream of coming home till he gets back. Most emphatic about it, he was. "I shan't have an easy moment", he says to me, "unless I know that my darling wife was under lock and key." Those were his words: "My darling wife," he said. Oh, he is comical, that Robin! So mind you do what he says, else poor old Dolly is going to get it in the neck.'

'I don't mind staying,' I said. 'I feel a bit limp, as it happens.'

'You look it, dear. White as a sheet. Gave me quite a turn. What a thing to do! No wonder your poor boy gets so het up about you!'

'How did you get here?' I asked. 'Surely you didn't lug all that lot on the bus?'

'Oh no, dear; Bert brought me over in the car. He's to take a few things down to the Treasure Trove and then come back for me.'

'Aunt Moo sent you in the Princess?' I asked in amazement. 'My condition must be more serious than they've let on.'

'Well, there were all these things to take to Mrs Zany, and then, you see, dear, your poor Auntie's ever so worried about the hospital diet, so she wanted you to have all this patty and stuff. She said the hospital food might do all right, if you were really ill, but with this clump on the head what you need is building up. Not that a clump on the head is anything to be sneezed at, as I told her. I've known them turn very nasty.'

The pervasive smell of hospital disinfectant had gone to Dolly's head like new wine and she prattled on, describing the numerous stricken friends and relatives she had visited, right here, in these very walls where she was talking to me now, many of whom had been clumped on the head, as they hadn't thought anything about at the time. It was only weeks later that they'd experienced this burning agony, or found themselves paralysed from the waist down.

However, among the many sad anecdotes from the near and distant past, there were two to which I paid more than token attention, and the first concerned Christabel. Dolly informed me that she had been to see her, before coming to me, and had got the fright of her life.

'Yes, she gave me the fright of my life, too. It was the last thing I remember, before I got my clump on the head. How is she?'

'Oh, cheeky as you please! Told me she expected to be out in a day or two. She's a card, that Miss Blake, she really is.'

'How did you get past the gorgon on the door?"

'The what, dear?'

'The policewoman.'

'Oh, her! Yes, Sister told me about her, but she went off duty at eight o'clock. They'll be sending another one up, any minute, she seemed to think. Not best pleased about it, either. I could tell that, by the way she spoke. And what good they think they'll do with that beats me, as I said to her. Miss Blake would just as likely jump out of the window as not, if the fit took her.'

The second item which aroused a spark of interest had occurred outside the hospital and the victim, in this case, was Anabel's dog. He had suffered a clump on the head in the form of a bullet between the eyes and had been found, stiff and dead, in the paddock which separated Mill Cottage from the Haverford Court woods.

'But, Dolly, who could have done such a thing?'

'Oh, there's plenty round here taking out guns as don't know how to use them. Cousin of mine got shot in the leg once, by someone as was supposed to be aiming at a pheasant. Got off scot free, too. Some of these magistrates don't give a hoot.'

'But this is not the season for pheasants.'

'Well, there's this tale about a roe deer being on the move, and some of them taking a rifle to look for it. Might account for it.'

'Yes, that sounds a bit more like it, but I still don't see how they could mistake a dog for a deer, at that range.'

'No, and it doesn't do to believe everything you hear, as your Auntie's so fond of saying. Now, what's up with Bert, I wonder? Oh, there he is! Sitting out in the yard like Patience on a Monument. Never do to keep him waiting, or there won't half be ructions. Okey doke, then, dear; take care of yourself and don't go dancing about with that bad head.'

Dancing about with my bad head was precisely the programme I had in mind, for the news that Christabel's guard had been removed had inspired me to have another shot at getting into her room, while the coast was clear. However, Dolly had no sooner left, and provided me with the chance for this excursion, than I found myself overcome by lassitude and a deep reluctance to move a muscle. As though this were not discouraging enough, I soon became infected with another form of hospital malaise. This one has something in common with the queasiness which overtakes me when circling round Kennedy airport in a thunderstorm, and it struck me that cabin crews have picked up a few tips from the nursing profession, in the secretive and preoccupied manner in which they turn away questions.

On this occasion, there were no questions to be asked, at least out loud, for the people in charge were invisible; but the sounds of their activity in the passage outside evoked exactly the same uneasiness. A door close to mine opened and shut four times in a minute; and each time it opened my straining ears caught the urgent murmur of voices. This was followed by creakings and scufflings in the corridor and the sound of heavy objects being trundled past.

Soon, all the sounds died away, but the sudden hush brought no release of tension. Just as in the aircraft, I was tempted to ring for a glass of water, simply to establish human contact, but luckily this bold gesture was not called for. In the nick of time, O'Malley came charging in with my elevenses.

Her eyes literally popped when she saw Aunt Moo's stack of groceries, so I was able to unload most of them on her, to brighten up the Nurses' Canteen; and, after the most perfunctory pretence that the recent brouhaha had signified nothing out of the ordinary, she admitted that poor old Miss Blake had been the cause of it. She had given them all something to think about, by having a heart attack, within two minutes of swallowing her mid-morning cuppa.

'Oh, no! But how awful! She's not . . . ?'

'Now don't go getting excited, will you? She's being well looked after. We've moved her over to the intensive-care ward.'

'And will she be all right, really?'

'She still has plenty of fight left in her, I dare say,' was all that I could get from her.

(iii)

'By the way, how did your conference go?' I asked Robin, towards the end of the day.

He had arrived at the hospital hours after I had given him up, and had then been inclined to feel aggrieved because I was not ready to leave on the instant. However, I had pacified him by making quite a passable snack out of the remaining jar of homemade pate and some melba toast, which was all that was left of Aunt Moo's bounty, and had regaled him, as he ate it, with a description of my eventful day. The question came as a postscript to this recital.

'I can't claim to be black and blue from pats on the back,' he answered, 'but we struggled through.'

'We? You mean Colie boy was with you?'

'He came along for the ride. Anyway, the upshot was that I'm to stay put, until the picture gets a bit clearer.'

'Which picture? Or is there only one?'

'No, I think there must be two. It would be so neat to assume that Sir Maddox was on the scent of the robbery gang and that one of its members was also at the party and all set to bump him off. It won't work, though. There simply isn't a shred of evidence to support it.'

'So you believe it was suicide, after all?'

'No, far from it. I refuse to accept that a sane man would take his own life in such a way, at such a moment. Furthermore, if Brand was in a suicidal frame of mind that evening, then I don't know Christmas from Easter and I'm in the wrong profession.'

'So what is the alternative? Is it possible that he took the wrong pill by mistake? It was dark, after all, and he was pretty squiffy by that time.'

'Yes, but cyanide, Tessa! It's simply inconceivable. Only a madman would carry the stuff around on him, and you'd have to be worse than mad to conceal it among your indigestion pills, or whatever. Besides, there were several grains of poison in the dregs of his glass. So the dose must have been dropped into the tumbler, which is the method a murderer would have been obliged to use. If it had been self-administered, he'd have been more likely to swallow the stuff in one go, and send the vodka down as a chaser.'

'It's odd. though, isn't it?'

'Very. What, in particular?'

'The dose being actually in the drink and his not noticing it. I was always given to understand that vodka was practically tasteless. Why didn't he take one sip and spit it out? He can't have been that far gone in his cups.'

'No, but you're forgetting how he insisted on mixing it with that special brand of vermouth. I think the vodka obsession was really more of an ideological stunt than anything else, because the vermouth had such a strong flavour that it wouldn't have made much difference what you put with it. And, if he had gulped some down and then realised there was something wrong, he wouldn't have had much time to do anything about it. Death would have been practically instantaneous.'

'But he didn't even cry out or make choking noises, as far as anyone can tell. Christabel would have heard that. She may be blind, but she's not deaf.'

'Well, I have my theories about that, too; but, on the other hand, she might not have noticed. Everyone was groaning in undertones and flinging themselves around a bit, I shouldn't wonder. And the tape recorder was turned up so loud that it drowned out most other noises. No, it all points to murder, and the culprit has to be one of those five people incarcerated with him in the good old fun-room. I should think the Harper Barringtons would have to change its name after this, wouldn't you?'

'Yes, Rumpus does turn out to have been more suitable, after all.'

'So, there we are! One victim and five suspects, all together in a sealed room, as the saying goes, and not the whiff of a motive. Cole still insists that there must be a connection somewhere with the art gang, but I'm coming to the end of that particular road. It is too much to swallow that, by coming down here to nose out one crime, I set off another which was related to it. As though one's mere presence had acted as a kind of catalyst.'

'Cata what?'

'Lyst.'

'Thank you. And that reminds me; you've left one off yours. You said there were five suspects, but even excluding our party, I make it six.'

'You include Anabel? No, I hadn't overlooked her and I don't rule her out on grounds of youth, what's more. I imagine if a person has murderous tendencies they're just as likely to come out at sixteen as at any other age. It's simply lack of motive which puts her out of the running. She was clearly batty about her old Uncle Mad, and I simply don't believe her to be capable of putting on an act of that kind.'

'I agree with you there, but it's still possible that she was an unwilling accessory. She was certainly in the best position of all of us to see what everyone in the room was up to. In fact, it's a big surprise to me that it's Prince who's been shot, and not Anabel, herself.'

'And it's a big surprise to me that it should take you half an hour to get your face plastered up for a ten minute drive. I doubt if there'll be any photographers outside, you know. Cole has been at great pains to keep your little escapade dark.'

'Good old Cole,' I said bitterly. 'How did we ever live without him? Come on, then; let's go.'

I bade a tearful farewell to Nurse O'Malley, who, in twenty-four hours, had become my dearest friend in all the world, and she assured me that Christabel was doing as well as could be expected. However, as I had no idea what anyone had expected, the point was lost.

On the way home to The Towers, I reverted once more to the subject of Anabel's dog:

'Dolly may know more than she's told me, because she keeps her ear well to the ground, and she was certainly in a big hurry to get away all of a sudden when I started probing; but she did let it out that he can only have been dead for a few hours when they found him. So that means he was shot within half a mile of the barn at about the same time as I was there myself.'

'It doesn't necessarily follow that he was killed on the spot. He could have been shot first and dumped there after dark. You didn't hear anything, did you?'

'I have a vague memory of hearing shots in the distance, when I was walking towards the barn; but that's such a normal sound in those woods and it wouldn't have made any particular impression. Besides, I had other things on my mind.'

'So I gathered. Some day you must tell me what they were.'

'I will, if my theory is ever proved. Although that seems rather unlikely now. Listen, though, Robin, I've just had a crazy idea. Don't laugh, please! Do you suppose the murderer killed Prince as a not very subtle warning to Anabel to keep her mouth shut about anything she may have seen?'

'I'm not laughing,' Robin said gloomily. 'The same possibility occurred to me, as soon as you told me about it.'

THIRTEEN

(i)

THE next day was Saturday and, although Robin went bounding off to meet Cole, just as usual, the full tedium of another day at The Towers did not set in at once, owing to the arrival through the post of some compulsive reading-matter. It was contained in a package which Dolly delivered with my breakfast tray.

I had been intending to detain her for a little light conversation about the demise of a golden retriever, but the sight of my agent's label on the parcel instantly banished all such ideas.

In the hurly-burly of the past few days I had almost, though admittedly not quite, forgotten about the première of my last film, which had taken place a few days earlier in New York. My agent, ever watchful in these matters, had acquired copies of the local papers which had covered it, and had posted me the clippings. There was quite a batch of them, all long and mostly enthusiastic, but the size of the package was accounted for by the fact that, in one case, she had enclosed the whole magazine. I saw why, after I had waded through every word of the review, of which there was hardly a cross one. At the bottom of it, she had written in red ink: 'See Also P. 32.'

I obeyed with all speed and discovered that P. 32 was the week's Personality Page. There were seven names featured on this occasion and we all got two or three paragraphs. Mine was based on the fact that I was married to 'Scotland Yard's Up and Coming Robin Price', a circumstance which the writer evidently expected would send his eight million readers into a ferment of excitement.

He referred to me thereafter as 'Cinemactress Crichton' and to Robin as 'Husband Price'. I was quoted as saying that I found one of our British Policemen Wonderful and there was a photograph of us, grinning at each other in a restaurant, rather startlingly captioned 'Crichton in Custody'.

However, there is a theory that it never matters what they say so long as they say something, and I was quite dazzled by my agent's astuteness in sending me the magazine intact. It might be considered beyond the pale to scatter press cuttings over the coffee table, but no one could object to the current number of a celebrated periodical, even if it had been pressed out to fall open at a certain page; and I could hardly wait to see Husband Price's face, when his eye lighted on this potted biography.

Unfortunately, it was an experience which had to be postponed until lunch time, and as a temporary substitute Aunt Moo was practically useless. I did finally get her curiosity sharpened up to the pitch where she gathered the magazine into her lap, but it did not fall open at the right page, after all, and she became totally bogged down in a colour advertisement for an international airline. For some mysterious reason, they had chosen to promote their image not, as one might expect, with undertakings to fly from place to place in reasonable time and all engines turning over, but with proud boasts of the *haute cuisine* they dished up on the journey. One got the impression that they considered it almost worth the trouble of crossing the Atlantic in order to sample the menu, and Aunt Moo certainly took it in this spirit. After an interminable discussion about the trickiness of doling out lemon sorbet to two hundred passengers simultaneously, she announced that it would not be very practical, since one would presumably be required to pay the full fare, whether one accepted all eight courses, or made do with a paltry half-dozen.

I was bracing myself to enter the ring for the second round, when Dolly burst in with the news that Mr Robinson was on the telephone. Having been sent bursting out again to collect further particulars, she returned a few minutes later and announced that it was a private matter, not to be divulged to an intermediary. I could see that this had made a slight dent in Aunt Moo's armour, but Guy should have known that it required something pithier than that to get her on her feet.

There followed the time-honoured routine, with Dolly darting back and forth, until the breakthrough was achieved.

Still adamant in her refusal to leave her armchair, Aunt Moo consented to receive Mr Robinson, in person, at four o'clock that afternoon. Hearing this, I realised that her mind would thenceforth be given over exclusively to the question of chocolate buns, cucumber sandwiches, etcetera, to accompany this interview, and that hopes of planting some tiny seed of interest in the career of Cinemactress Crichton could now be classed as withered. So I let her ponder these weighty problems in silence, while I moodily skimmed through some of the other pages in the magazine.

Whatever Fates are in charge of these matters had certainly known a thing or two when they arranged for me to be born under the sign of Gemini. Injecting the blood stream with the acting bug had been a clever follow-up, for few professions call for a more determinedly dual personality. Conniving at, if not actually manipulating my marriage to Robin had put the seal on matters.

In dubbing me 'Copper's Moll', Christabel had uttered an exact half-truth, but it certainly did not describe my condition that morning. The other twin had taken over and, for the time being, I had no more interest in crime and detection than a child of two.

Instead of cogitating on the implications of this new development, I frittered away my time by rereading the film review; then turned back to skim through some of the other items in the Personality line-up. This brought me up to date with the activities of someone called Preacher Jones, who had lashed himself to the steeple of a church in Alabama; also of the ex-President of Consolidated United Trust Enterprises, Inc., who, after a disastrous skirmish with the Monopolies Board, concerning some dud takeover deal, had taken off for an unknown destination, much to the bewilderment of his fourth wife, ex-screen queen,

Constance Bellamy. I might add that he was made to look pretty silly by the next story, which featured some Sheik of Oilville, who had been snapped in a millionaire Dallas nite-spot, entwined in the arms of the young female who was about to become bride number eighty; but not once, as I absorbed all this improbable information, did it occur to me that Guy's insistence on a private conference with Aunt Moo might have some bearing on the murder.

It was left to Husband Price to draw the inference. Aunt Moo having by then retired to the kitchen to knock up a mayonnaise for the dressed crab, I seized the chance to get his undivided attention focused on the New York première. He had become accustomed, if not reconciled, to the actor's insatiable craving for reassurance, and oohed and ahed his way through the column in quite the proper spirit. Whereupon, with ego restored, I lost all interest in the subject and went straight on to tell him of the meeting which had been convened for four o'clock.

'Might be worth sitting in on it,' he remarked.

'Fat chance! This is top secret, as far as I can make out.'

'All the more reason,' replied Scotland Yard's Up and Coming Price.

'How do you mean? You're not suggesting it might have something to do with . . . ? Oh, Robin, do you honestly think so? What fun! Perhaps he intends to cook up some story and get Aunt Moo's backing for it.'

'Could be.'

'Well, I'll do my best to edge myself in, but it seems pretty hopeless. Guy would never be such a fool as to give himself away in front of me.'

'No, that's true.'

'So what are you suggesting? Not that I should eavesdrop?'

'Oh, ain't I?'

'I suppose it's worth a try,' I said thoughtfully, every inch the Copper's Moll, once more.

(ii)

By half-past three, while Aunt Moo was still at her siesta, I had brought my props onto the back verandah and set them out beside the half-open french windows. They consisted of a limp *gros point* canvas, to which I had been adding an intermittent stitch over the past fifteen years, some writing-paper and envelopes, and one of the bound copies of *Punch*. I was new to the game and had still to learn whether the pretence of reading, writing or sewing would be more conducive to the successful eavesdrop.

Guy made his entrance on the stroke of four, but, in the meantime, I had been privileged to overhear the prologue, which was also a form of dress rehearsal. It consisted of a brief scene between Aunt Moo and Dolly and there was any amount of business with lace tablecloths, silver teapots, etcetera, before, apparently, the scenery satisfied Aunt Moo's exigent standards.

I say 'apparently', because at first I failed to make out a single word that either of them said; and this deficiency did not improve in the case of Aunt Moo. On the other hand, I found that, by shifting my chair this way and that, I was able to tune into Dolly from time to time. This was satisfactory, because it was not Aunt Moo's responses that I was most keen to hear and, given Guy's professional diction, I considered myself not badly situated to pick up some pointers.

'Good afternoon, my dear Mrs Hankinson,' I heard him say. He was using the unctuous clergyman voice for this occasion, a choice which I applauded, both on artistic and practical grounds. It harmonised with the set and gave maximum audibility.

'. . . .'

These dots represent Aunt Moo's reply, and will be used for that purpose throughout the ensuing dialogue. Even when I could distinguish her words, they were invariably too far off the point to be worth including in the records.

'Thank you. And how scrumptious they look! May I help myself? I am afraid I have bad news to relate, dear lady.'

'. . . . Yes, two lumps, please. The fact is, we appear to have been a little ah . . . um . . . over-optimistic in our assessment, and we wondered if you could see your way. . . . Oh, thank you, I will have another. . . . Yes, perfectly genuine; there was no mistake there . . . mainly that his work is out of fashion at the moment. Xenia telephoned. . . . Sothebys. . . . they had advised her to put a reserve of two fifty on the lot.'

'. . . .'

'Yes, laughable . . . thoroughly agree. The point is. . . .'

'. . . .'

'No more, thank you . . . tiny slice, if you insist . . . whether we could make some adjustment in the original price . . . so very glad to have your opinion.'

I should have been moderately glad of it, too, but, infuriatingly enough, the next voice I heard was Dolly's. Exactly how and when she had got into the act was a mystery. There was no mistaking that she was in a state of harassment beyond the norm, but nevertheless there are some words which contrive to be audible, even in the most adverse conditions and they include one's own name. Unfortunately, in craning forward to catch what was being said about me, I knocked my chair against the table and sent the volume of *Punch* shooting on to the stone terrace. A second later, the french window was flung wide open and Guy stood framed inside it.

I knew him to be capable of smart reactions, but he must really have come at the gallop this time, and the exertion had quite shaken him out of his normal imperturbability. He stood rigid, in the doorway, breathing deeply through parted lips, and two hard lines had etched themselves from nose to mouth. His eyes were hard as pebbles and no one had ever looked less like an unctuous clergyman.

'Oh, hallo!' I said uncertainly. 'Fancy meeting you!'

He was spared the necessity of capping this brilliant opening, because Dolly had caught up with him and was scuffling about in the background, drying to attract my attention. Becoming aware of this, Guy turned and walked away, still without a word.

'It's Matron, dear,' Dolly panted. 'On the phone. Oh dear, I feel quite frantic. I've been searching all over the place for you, in your room and everywhere. I'm afraid she'll have rung off, by now. Hasn't got a minute to live, by the sound of it. Run along and call her back, there's a dear, otherwise I'll be in hot water. She's got something very urgent to tell you about Miss Blake.'

'May I have the car this evening, Aunt Moo? I have to go to the hospital to see Christabel. It seems she's been asking for me.'

'Sure, and oy'll droive you there, meself,' Guy said. 'It's on me way.'

He was stretched out in an armchair and, in the ten minutes which had elapsed since our previous encounter, had regained every shred of his composure.

'That's sweet of you, Guy, but they don't want me until six. They say she's pretty well doped at the moment, but they expect her to be thinking more clearly in an hour or two. Still, on second thoughts, if it's really on your way, you could drop me off there. It might be a good idea to wait around and catch her at the right moment.'

Aunt Moo smiled her secretive, cat-like smile and dealt herself a hand of Demon Patience. I suspected her of being so relieved that the Princess was not to be sullied by a ten-minute drive that she even forgot to warn me about being late for dinner.

FOURTEEN

(i)

THERE was a call-box in the hospital foyer, as I knew from previous visits, and I went inside and dialled Haverford Police Station. It took ages to run Robin to earth, but there was plenty to look at while I waited.

It was evidently the day for the post-natal clinic, for I could see through to the waiting-room and it was crowded with young mothers, perpetually twitching at their babies' shawls and casting sidelong glances at the rival progeny.

The foyer itself was a sea of prams and portable cots, and a handful of slightly older children were clambering about among them. They were regularly reprimanded for this by passing members of the hospital staff, who chivvied them back to their mothers, but they soon came zooming in again, and I even saw one three-year-old delinquent grab a bar of chocolate from a trolley like the one I had seen Nancy with the day before.

'Hallo!' Robin said at last. 'Where are you?'

I told him, adding: 'They say Christabel is still asleep, but they're going to let me know the minute she's visible.

Anyway, I thought it would be a smart move to ring you from here. The Towers telephone is a bit public.'

'Does that mean you have something to report?'

'Not a lot, I'm afraid, and not very gristy to the mill.'

After describing the snatches I had picked up from my verandah spy-post, I went on:

'So, you see, it doesn't look as though I'm cut out for the espionage game; although between them Christabel and Dolly would have put a spoke in anyone's wheel. Also, Robin, their conference obviously wasn't related to the murder. It simply confirmed our theory that Aunt Moo is quietly disposing of Uncle Andrew's possessions and the Robinsons are taking a rake-off.'

'Yes. Sorry you had to risk your reputation for nothing.'

'It wasn't quite nothing. In fact, darling, the interesting thing – Oh, just a minute. I'll tell you later. I've got to go now.'

I had been about to give a dramatic account of Guy's disproportionately violent reaction to my presence, but Nurse O'Malley had appeared in the hall, and I guessed from her flashing glances that Christabel was now ready to see me.

No guess could have been further from the mark, for it turned out that Christabel would never be in a position to see anyone again. O'Malley related the facts in a little cubby-hole of a room, unfurnished except for a shabby old sink and glass cupboards full of drugs and dressings.

'Now, you must try not to upset yourself, you know. Poor old dear, it was just as well she did go. Her right side took a regular beating in that fire. She'd not have been fit for her painting or anything else, the state she was in.'

'What was it?' I asked. 'Another heart attack?'

'Just a wee one, but she wouldn't have known a thing about it. Passed away in her sleep, poor lady.'

'Will there be a post mortem?'

She had evidently been unprepared for this and looked somewhat flustered:

'Now that's not a thing we need to go bothering our heads about, is it? That's for the authorities to say. What we have to think about is how to get you safely home to your Auntie's. Will I give her a ring and ask her to send the car down?'

'Have the police been told about Christabel yet?'

She assumed the self-consciously casual expression which accompanies an extra-energetic shake of the thermometer, saying:

'Oh, they'll be told soon enough. Now, how about a nice cup of tea to perk you up, while I get on the phone?'

'No, I'm all right. I was only thinking that, if the police had been told, Robin will know about it by now and he'll be on his way here. So I could go home with him.'

'Great heavens above! The woman's a genius! And what's the betting you're right? Just sit tight, now, for a few minutes, and I shouldn't be surprised to see him rolling up before you can say Jack Robinson.'

'Or Guy Robinson, or Xenia Robinson, came to that,' I said, when relating these matters on the homeward journey. 'Anyway, darling old O'Malley fell smack into my trap, and I realised that the police certainly had been informed of Christabel's death. Which leads me to suppose that somebody, somewhere, is not satisfied that it was a natural one. Correct?'

'Too early to say. There'll have to be a post mortem, of course. To go back to all those Robinsons for a moment: I thought you told me on the telephone that the conversation you overheard was relatively harmless?'

'So it was, and, as far as he was concerned, it could have been completely innocent. Even supposing he has been helping her to unload some of Uncle Andrew's possessions, that would be quite a normal thing for someone in his line of business. He may not know that, legally, they're not hers to dispose of. So why is he in such a tantrum when he finds I've been listening in?'

'You're sure that was his reaction? Not over-dramatising things in retrospect, by any chance?'

'What a suggestion! No, I'm positive, Robin. It was genuine anger and panic, too, I shouldn't wonder. I'd really have been scared, if Dolly hadn't been there.'

'Though not too scared to drive to the hospital with him, ten minutes later?'

'No, that's true, but he'd got a hold of himself by then. There's nothing faintly sinister about him in the ordinary way, is there? Besides, I was thinking more about Christabel, by that time. I was all worked up about why the things she had to tell me had become so urgent all of a sudden. And now I shall never know, I suppose.'

'And on the drive to the hospital did Guy allude to the other thing? Try to pump you about what you might have overheard, for instance?'

'Not really. He said something vague about old people getting curious fixations and what not, but he was all soft soap and treacle at that point. Pretended to be very concerned about Christabel, too; and he was madly quizzy about her wanting to see me. It was quite a lark, really.'

'Was it? Why?'

'Because I can put on an act, too, when I want to; and I made out I was just as much in the dark as he was.'

'Well, you were, and still are, surely?'

'Not on your life!'

'Oh, come now! A minute ago I heard you say, "And now I shall never know."'

'Not true, Robin. I said I should never know what had made it so urgent. That's still a puzzle, unless, of course, she knew she was dying and wanted to cleanse her soul; but that doesn't really fit with Christabel. On the whole, I incline to the view that she had every intention of recovering.'

'Cleanse her soul by confessing to the murder?'

'Oh, dear me, no. Although, as it happens, it was something which gave her a first-class motive; and she may have begun to realise that I would soon see that for myself, and maybe pass the facts on to you.'

We were within a hundred yards of The Towers, as I spoke, but Robin pulled the car into the side of the road and switched off the engine.

'If so,' he said, 'it sounds to me as though she over-estimated you. You still haven't explained about that mad excursion to the barn, and presumably it's tied up with these hints you're throwing out now. But let's get things straight, Tessa. If you know or suspect something. which Christabel knew or suspected, that relates in any way to the murder, you must tell me about it and stop fooling around. It's not merely your duty to do so, it's your own safety that I'm even more concerned about.'

'Oh, why, Robin? Do you imagine that Christabel has now been killed because of this knowledge or suspicion of hers? That's absolutely out, I promise you. Besides, O'Malley assured me it was a straightforward heart attack.'

'Maybe, but we're not prepared to take Nurse O'Malley's word for it just yet. There have been too many oddities about Christabel's behaviour and it's becoming hourly more apparent that you're mixed up in whatever game she was playing. Now, for the last time, are you going to come clean, or aren't you?'

'Keep your wool on! Of course, I am.'

'Good. Then now's the time. And do try, just for once, to begin at the beginning.'

Just for once, I did so.

(ii)

'It all began before the murder, you know; exactly a week ago, in fact. You remember Christabel's burglary and how cagey she got when you advised her to report it?'

'Indeed, I do. It was one reason for saying that she's been acting funny all along. I never could decide whether she invented it and, if so, why.'

'There have been too many burglaries, that's the trouble,' I told him. 'It has clouded our vision, because some are connected and some are not. Just count them. Leaving aside the kind of armchair racket, which Aunt Moo seems to be conducting, we started with the one at Sir Maddox's flat, which brought you down here.'

'Followed by Christabel's contribution, which may or may not have been genuine.'

'Oh, I'm sure it was, and that's where the connections start, because there was a similar episode, the following night, at Haverford Court.'

'Immediately after the murder, in fact.'

'Yes; and note the parallels. Once again the thief went to some trouble to break into premises where there were stacks of valuables lying around, and appears to have gone away empty-handed.'

'And where does all that lead you?'

'To the conclusion that it wasn't valuables he was after?'

'What, then?'

'Evidence.'

Robin lifted his hands off the steering-wheel and turned round to shake his head at me:

'No, that won't do. The murder hasn't been committed when Christabel's thief made his call. So he can hardly have been looking for evidence at that stage.'

'Not evidence of murder; I don't mean that, although there is a kind of motive tucked away in all this, which is why I have hesitated to pass my findings on. But it can't hurt her, now she's dead.'

'You sound pretty confident, Tessa; but let's face it, your findings, as you call them, can only be surmise. Christabel died before you had a chance to talk to her, so how can you actually know anything?'

'But I do,' I protested. 'And Christabel knew that I knew. No talking was necessary. The mere fact of her sending for me proved it.'

'Proved what? I rather wish I hadn't been so insistent on your starting at the beginning. It might have been better if you had stuck to your usual method of plunging in somewhere around the middle. Just tell me what it was that Christabel had to say to you, and which you already knew.'

'In a word, that it was Sir Maddox who broke into the barn.'

'That's quite a word, I must admit; and, if it's the middle, I'd just as soon you began at the end. What the hell would he do a thing like that for?'

'To steal some of her paintings. I'm not sure how many. Two or three, maybe.'

'It's a relief to hear there's something you're not sure of. Of all the crazy notions! And how do you account for the fact that Christabel was so keen to hush it up? She loathed

Brand, didn't she? It would have been a splendid stick to beat him with.'

'A double-edged one, unfortunately, so she couldn't use it. All she could do was to get the stolen pictures back again, as fast as she could and with the minimum of fuss.'

'Forgive my saying so, but I should have thought the bigger the fuss the faster she'd have got them back?'

'In other circumstances that might be so, but it had to be done without anyone examining the pictures and without their knowing who'd pinched them. Otherwise, he would have retaliated by exposing her to a jeering world for the old fraud that she was.'

'Really? And what sort of old fraud was that?'

'I don't know the technical name, but it's the one who passes off spurious works of art as genuine. Those pictures weren't painted by Mott at all. She did them herself. At least, not the whole lot, but most of them, and certainly those which Maddox took away.'

'With what object, for God's sake? If what you say is true, they would have no particular value.'

'That wasn't the attraction. What he wanted was to get such a hold over Christabel that she would have been completely in his power. Giving up Mill Cottage would doubtless have been his first demand. And, so long as she toed the line, he probably wouldn't have given her away. Much more fun to keep the threat of exposure hanging over her head.'

'I should love to hear how you arrived at these extraordinary conclusions.'

'Well, to begin with –'

'No,' Robin said, 'if you don't mind, I'll begin this time. First tell me what possible reason she could have had for passing off her own work as Mott's, and then how she managed to get away with it?'

'Well, it might not count as a reason for any thoroughly sane person, but she was a bit cracked, in some respects. Possibly, she was always a bit eccentric and the life she led with old Mott made her a sight worse. That's guessing, because it was before my time; but it is a fact that a lot of people are now getting around to the idea that she was very talented, in her own right. I maintain that she always was. I can't believe that a flair of that kind, in someone perpetually surrounded by artists and artists' materials, would have stayed dormant until she was pushing seventy. In the early days, I expect she learnt a lot from Mott and was influenced by him, but then I think it must have dawned on him how very good she was getting, and, mean-spirited old beast that he was, he became frightfully jealous. She never had a single exhibition and nobody ever saw her work when he was alive, and yet there's stacks of it piled up in her studio alone, far more than one person could have produced in three or four years.'

'Then why put up with it? They weren't married. She could have cut loose and branched out on her own any time she liked.'

'I know, but she was besotted about the old bastard. Everyone agrees on that. He was her whole life and, although he made sure that she had no artistic standing of her own, she did bask in his reflected glory and hobnobbed with the cream of the art world. That was specially true in the last years, when he was so dependent on her. Well, you can see what would happen as soon as he died?'

'Bang goes the power and the glory?'

'Yes, and I think she must have resented that; specially since they weren't married and he only left her a pittance.

I suppose she could have concentrated on her own work, at that point, but it's a bit rough to start building up a reputation when you're over sixty, and going blind into the bargain. I think she preferred the easier distinction of making herself sole custodian of more than half his life's output; ninety per cent of that, of course, having been compiled by herself during the thirty years they lived together. She even spread a few romantic tales about having stolen the pictures, when he was on his death bed, presumably in case it should occur to anyone that it was somewhat out of character for him to have bequeathed her such a goldmine.'

'But the snag about all this, Tessa, as I've said before, is that she simply couldn't have got away with it.'

'My darling, she did get away with it. I don't suggest that she tried to sell any of the paintings. She'd soon have got her comeuppance, if she had. But they were good enough and near enough to his style to fool the casual observer, even a knowledgeable one. The point is that money wasn't her object.'

'Just prestige?'

'In a crackpot kind of way, yes; people deferring to her, asking her advice and so on. Even people like the Harper Barringtons, who would have despised her in the ordinary way, worshipped at the Mott shrine; and galleries and things made a great fuss of her. Naturally, whenever she did consent to lend them anything she made jolly certain it was the genuine article.'

'Since she was so crafty about it, how did you manage to find her out?'

'There were three pointers. One came from Christabel, herself, another from Sir Maddox and the last from Toby.'

'Toby? What does he know about it?'

'Pretty well everything I've just told you, I imagine. I'll come to him in a moment. Maddox was the first one to see through the sham, and that was at the bottom of his snide remarks to her at the party; not teasing her about Russia, as we thought, but about her fake paintings, two or three of which were already in his possession. I don't know how he caught on, but that may not have been the first of his midnight swoops. Only, on the last occasion, he gave himself away by leaving his lighter behind.'

'His lighter? How do you know? Is that what you went to the barn to look for?'

'Oh no, Christabel had already found it. It had no significance for me at the time, but when you were out in the barn that morning she told me that you wouldn't find any cigarette ends, because she knew for a fact that the burglar was a non-smoker.'

'Rather a curious fact to base your premise on, if you don't mind my saying so.'

'I don't at all, because the answer only came to me in an upside down kind of way. You see, when I had my little brush with Maddox, he told me that he never smoked, but he offered me a cigarette from a gold case which he always carried. It was part of the old-world gallantry act that he liked to put on. He also told me that he normally carried a lighter, as well. Now who but a non-smoker could lose his lighter and have no clear idea of where or when? It was what first gave me the idea that he had used it to light his way through the barn, put it down somewhere and, not being in the habit of retrieving it automatically, had walked off without it. Christabel found it and put two and two together.'

'And promptly took counter measures, by breaking into the Court to steal back her own property?'

'That's my theory, yes. Not many people would have had the presence of mind to do such a thing within a few hours of his being murdered; but she was a bit fanatical on that subject. And really, you know, Robin, it was the best possible moment, with the master of the house safely dead and half the local constabulary gathered round the corpse. The snag was . . .'

'That she could have set it up for herself in just that way? Killed him at the party and later removed the evidence of a motive. It's not a bad idea.'

'There! I knew you'd take that attitude.'

'I haven't taken any attitude, I promise you; but if all you've told me is true it certainly bears further investigation. On the other hand, we'd look a bit silly if it turned out that every single picture in the barn was a bona fide Mott.'

'You'll have trouble establishing that, one way or the other. Most of what's left is in a frightful state. However, you could get an expert to examine the one you'll find among Christabel's belongings at the hospital. I only had time to snatch one, unfortunately.'

'Oh, I see! So that's what you were after?'

'Yes.'

'And Christabel caught you in the act and realised what you were up to?'

'Yes, it was bad luck, but I suppose she'd nipped out to make sure that the fire had made a thorough job of it, before the insurance people got too nosey.'

'And, afterwards, she deliberately hung onto your bag, containing the evidence you'd collected?'

'You'll go far, Robin.'

'Not without your assistance, it seems. For instance, who set fire to the barn, and why? Or haven't you wrapped that up yet?'

'You wrapped it up, yourself. You said that Christabel did it, and you were right; only it wasn't accidental.'

'Not a very logical action, in view of all the trouble she'd been to.'

'No, but it may have made her see how vulnerable she was. If Maddox saw through the trick, why shouldn't someone else? On the other hand, she obviously didn't intend to explode the myth; so, having retrieved the pictures from Haverford Court, she sent the whole shooting-match up in flames. She wasn't a very efficient pyromaniac, though, and the fire must have spread much more quickly than she had anticipated. Obviously, she meant to rescue all the genuine Motts and leave the rest to burn. Unfortunately for her, she left it a little too late and got badly burnt herself.'

'Well, all her belongings at the hospital will be with the police by now, so we may be able to prove something from the one you pinched. I'll talk to Cole about it, as soon as we get to The Towers. One other thing, though.'

'Yes?'

'You mentioned Toby.'

'Oh yes, he's fiendish, isn't he, the way he catches on, without even trying? He came into the library one morning, when I was fooling around with some Mott reproductions. He's a much better draughtsman than I am, and he knocked off something which looked passably authentic in about two minutes. It showed me conclusively how easy it would be for a trained artist to make a first-rate job of it. I fancy he got the same idea, too, and that was one reason why he was in such a tearing hurry to be off.'

'Before he became involved, I suppose?'

'Specially as he'd given you such a graphic word-picture of Christabel as the murderer. That was a big joke, of course, when he was wound up and over-excited. I imagine it became a lot less funny when he found he'd uncovered a genuine motive. He was fond of Christabel, after all. He wouldn't have wanted to get her into any trouble and he was probably terrified of coming out with something to put you on the right track.'

'Curious standard of ethics obtaining in your family. I've noticed it before. I wonder if Aunt Moo is similarly affected?'

'It begins to look as though they obtain more with her than anywhere else,' I admitted sadly.

Fifteen

Toby came back for Christabel's funeral, which was noble of him, though I doubt if he would have done so had he known more than the bare facts which I relayed on the telephone. Between that and his arrival the following day, Robin told me that an autopsy had been inevitable, since Christabel's own doctor had not been in attendance. It proved to be a sensible precaution, because the results showed that she had died from a small dose of potassium cyanide.

'So I am afraid your analysis was all too true, Tessa, and now I expect you're kicking yourself for having told me. Try not to think of it in that way, though. She's out of it now, and it's better that the truth should be faced than have innocent people under a cloud of suspicion for the rest of their lives.'

'Innocent, my foot!' I said, endeavouring to control myself. 'I'm damn sure that one of them isn't. Am I to take it that you're treating this as suicide, brought on by remorse?'

'I'm afraid you are.'

'The remorse part being for the murder of old Brand?'

'Among other things. There'll be an inquest, but I'd say the verdict is a foregone conclusion. The game was up and she knew it.'

'That doesn't sound a bit like Christabel. She was a fighter to the last ditch.'

'Maybe it wasn't only guilty conscience. There was also the fact that she'd been pretty badly injured. It was by no means certain that she'd have been able to paint again, or even look after herself properly.'

'She never looked after herself properly,' I retorted. 'And, as for losing the use of her right arm, that doesn't signify either. It may have escaped your notice, but she happens to have been left-handed.'

Robin looked distinctly shaken by this, and I rammed home the argument: 'I'll tell you another thing; if she had been planning suicide, why send out that urgent call for me? There wouldn't be much point, if she intended to be dead by the time I got there.'

'I think that can be explained. She was heavily sedated most of the time; probably forgot what she'd said two minutes afterwards. In that semi-hallucinatory state, she may easily have imagined that she'd confessed everything to you and the job was finished. Besides, Tessa, look at it this way: what else could it be? Nobody swallows cyanide by mistake. We went all through that with Brand. The third alternative is even more fantastic. You can't seriously imagine a totally unauthorised person strolling into her room and handing her a dose of cyanide, which she obligingly drank?'

'If she was as doped as you say, I don't see why not. And it wouldn't have to be a totally unauthorised person,' I added, struck by another memory. 'Incidentally, Robin, I take it there wasn't a nurse in the room at the time?'

'Well, no,' he admitted uncomfortably. 'Of course, there wasn't. It was unlucky that she should have been left alone, I agree, but that hospital is wickedly understaffed, just like all the rest of them; and you could argue that there was really no need for a continuous watch. She'd been sleeping peacefully only fifteen minutes before.'

'There'd been a fairly continuous watch the day before, as I happen to know.'

'But that was mainly to prevent her doing another walk-out. The circumstances had altered. She was recovering remarkably well from her heart attack, but there wasn't the faintest chance of her even being able to get out of bed without assistance.'

'So the poison, wherever it was hidden, must have been within reach?'

'Must have been.'

'Have they found out where she might have kept it?'

'The room was searched, naturally, but no more of the stuff came to light. That doesn't prove anything.'

'No, it doesn't.'

'I do understand your feelings, honestly, Tessa. She was a friend of yours and it's not a pleasant thing to learn about anyone; but I don't think you should allow prejudice to blind you to the facts. It's not like you.'

'It's just that I can't stand the jaunty way you blame her for everything. I don't mind about her taking her own life, if she felt it was best. She was old and alone and there was no one on earth who would have been harmed by her death; but, whether she did or not, it doesn't automatically follow that she was a murderess as well. I'm surprised that you can't see that and I think it's you who are the blind one. You're blindly toeing the line the real murderer has laid down for you, and thinking exactly as he intended you to.'

'And who would he be?'

'Oh, God knows. Anyone you like. I suppose Dolores is in the clear, because she'd bolted long before Christabel died, but she's the only one. With Dolly broadcasting it around, everyone in the neighbourhood would have known that Christabel was asking for me, with urgent information to impart. What more likely than that the murderer assumed that she had some damning evidence against him, and wanted me to pass it on to you?'

'Yes, that's feasible, and it would be quite in the character of the average murderer, but the overwhelming objection remains. How could he have got into her room? This has been checked up hill and down dale and it's an irrefutable fact that she wasn't on her own for more than fifteen minutes. No visitors called during that period, except yourself. It was physically impossible, as I've said before, for any unauthorised person to have got within miles of her.'

'Then I think it's high time they checked on the authorised people, for a change. I'm sorry to be obstinate about this, Robin, but it's all too pat and perfect. Furthermore, a lot more than this will be needed to persuade me that Christabel was capable of murder. I haven't got many strong convictions, and I'm not going to be shaken out of the few I do have.'

Robin was looking thoughtful, and I began to hope that he was veering round to my point of view, but he said sombrely:

'I'm afraid we're going to have to shake you out of this one. I had hoped to convince you without it, because, God knows, I've no wish to spoil your memories of her; but there are strong indications that she was fully capable of murder. So much so that she was even prepared to have a go at you.'

'What on earth do you mean?'

'We've had a closer look at those X-rays of yours. It was Cole's idea. He doesn't miss many tricks, and it struck him that there might be something not quite satisfactory about your injuries.'

'How brilliant of him!' I said. 'Not quite satisfactory is exactly the phrase which covers it.'

'In the sense that it might not have been an accident at all. When the radiologist showed us the photographs the first time, he was naturally only concerned to point out how the blows had missed this and that vital spot, so that your skull wasn't fractured, and you wouldn't be noticeably dottier than before. He wasn't in the least curious, and neither were we at that stage, about what kind of implement had caused the damage.'

'Implement?'

'That's right. As I say, it was Cole's idea and it was a winner. There's little doubt that what knocked you out in the first round was not falling bricks and masonry, but our old friend the blunt instrument. A bit of lead piping, or an iron bolt from one of the crates; something like that.'

'I don't believe it, Robin. Christabel would never do such a thing. Besides, she was unconscious when you found us. She couldn't have faked that.'

'No, but Cole's theory is that either she, in lunging forward to strike you, or else you, in falling, set up some pretty formidable vibrations in that shaky structure. That's what brought the bricks and rubble down, and they knocked her out, as well.'

'And have you found this famous blunt instrument?'

'Not to identify, no. As you can imagine, we weren't too particular about inspecting each separate bit of debris, at the time. We were in quite a hurry to get you out and it got flung around in all directions. But we've since found a number of things in the vicinity which would have served the purpose. Unfortunately, Christabel's hands were bandaged, so it would have been a waste of time to look for prints.'

'The tiresome thing is,' I said, 'that I'm still so hazy about what happened between Christabel walking into the barn, looking like an Egyptian mummy, and waking up outside on the grass. Perhaps, if they gave me one of those fancy drugs, I might do a total recall.'

Robin shook his head: 'I should drop that idea, if I were you. It might make things even worse for you. I'm sorry about this, truly, darling; but, you see, you're the one who's driven the last nail in her coffin, so to speak.'

'I have? How? Did I say something when I was unconscious? You should know better than to take that seriously.'

'Oh no, you were conscious all right; and you said it a minute ago. The thing is, we were a little bit troubled by the fact that Christabel's right arm was too weak to swing anything heavier than a match stick. For some God knows what reason, Cole and I both assumed that a painter would be right-handed. Isn't that weird? Anyway, you've now smoothed out that little snag for us.'

'There must be some mistake,' I muttered. 'There simply has to be.'

I went on muttering it, at intervals, for the next two days. There had to be some mistake and, somehow or other, I had to find out what it was.

This would probably have been my mood, in any case, for it was a constant and disagreeable reminder that my own words had been used to wrap up the case against Christabel. It presented me with the absolute duty not to give up until she was vindicated. The fact that the latest charge against her stemmed from Superintendent Cole merely clinched the matter.

SIXTEEN

'ONE thing to do,' I said, 'is to try and recall every word and incident remotely connected with the murders.'

'It sounds a fearful task and I don't remember any of it being particularly scintillating even at the time.'

'We are not here to amuse ourselves,' I pointed out, 'and it stands to reason that the guilty party must have given himself away, at one point, if only we could go back and find it.'

'If you say so,' Toby sighed.

Once more, I had enlisted him as my unwilling accomplice, and the unwillingness did not bother me particularly. The mere fact that, unlike Robin, he had reservations about Christabel's guilt in the three little matters of murder, grievous bodily harm and suicide was all I needed. He had known her longer than any of us and his qualified opinion that she was not the violent type had given me real hope of proving that the police were barking up the wrong tree, but had been manoeuvred into the wrong part of the wood.

However, I was careful to inquire on what he based his judgement, lest it should turn out that the single circumstance in her favour was that everyone else believed her to be guilty.

'I suppose it might have something to do with her being an artist,' he had admitted. 'I could be prejudiced, you know, but I have always found them to be more fundamentally balanced than most other people. For one thing, the world allows them a certain licence in non-conformity, which must be very healthy for the psyche, but there's also this thing of being able to sink all their moods and passions in their work. I think this is specially true of painters and sculptors, who have to use all that physical, as well as mental, energy while they're at it. Hark at me!'

'I do hark and I consider that you have made a valid point. It has always seemed to me that when Christabel discovered that Sir Mad had unearthed her secret, she did the most practical thing in the world, which was to steal back the evidence he had collected and destroy it. Going around killing people and clumping people on the head was simply asking for trouble and a complete waste of effort. Now, I maintain that the individual we are looking for has to be someone who is emotionally twisted up and therefore given to rash and ill-considered gestures.'

'There must be plenty of those about.'

'But, luckily, we only have to consider five. Two Robinsons and three Harper Barringtons.'

'Three?'

'Yes. Robin struck Anabel off, but she is older than she looks, you know. I think her mother may have deliberately kept her back, probably from jealousy. In fact, she is nearly seventeen, and who knows how many fantasies and frustrations are seething behind those vapid features?'

'I suppose we can assume that a few are, but that's hardly the point, and neither is her age. There are three things to eliminate her, in my opinion. One is that we were all in a position to see that she didn't go near her Uncle Mad, after they had supplied him with that fearful concoction which quite understandably killed him. The second is lack of motive. The third, and most damning, from your point of view, is that she would have run up against the little problem of acquiring enough cyanide to kill three adults.'

'I'll take your points in order. In the first place, we couldn't absolutely swear that she didn't slide out for a moment, while that ghastly film was running. She'd obviously sat through it, doing her stunt with the tape recorder, dozens of times, and would have known exactly when it was safe to leave it for a second or two. Strictly speaking, there were only two people who could say with certainty whether she did or not; one was Uncle Maddox and the other was Christabel, and I find that highly significant. Point number two: so far we haven't found a motive for anyone, unless you count Christabel's, which I don't, so she's in the same boat as everyone else, as far as that goes. As for getting hold of supplies of cyanide, I can only say quite simply that I'm working on it.'

'And I can only say quite simply that you'll have your work cut out.'

'I know it,' I sighed, 'but the same applies to all my lovely suspects. Whichever line I follow only leads straight into a brick wall. I had hopes of Roger, at one time. At least he seemed to have some kind of a motive, the way old Maddox was fooling around with his daughter; but now Robin tells me she isn't his daughter at all, and one could hardly hope for a stepfather to feel so sensitive, could one? The case against Nancy is even more of a washout. I know that she had the best opportunity of all, but what possible reason could there be? She was dotty about him; and the idea of her going to such lengths to protect Anabel, even supposing she knew what was going on, is simply not credible. She could have found a million ways to put a stop to it.'

'Unless she was in love with the old monster herself, and snuffed him in a fit of jealous rage.'

'It's not a bad idea, Toby, and I've toyed with it myself, but on the whole I'm beginning to feel that the Robinsons are our best bet.'

'Singly, or together?'

'I haven't decided yet, but there's something fishy about that set up. I've felt it all along. And, if it does turn out that there's a connection between the murder and Robin's art thefts, that shop of theirs would make an awfully good sorting house for the gang.'

'Which art thefts?'

'I wasn't supposed to mention that, but I don't suppose the ban is in operation now. He originally came down here because things pointed to a gang of thieves having their headquarters in this neighbourhood. So far as I know, he hasn't got to first base with that idea, but it would be fun if we could tie it up for him and throw in a murderer, as well.'

'The theory being that the Robinsons are part of the gang?'

'And killed Sir Maddox because he was on to them; later moving on to Christabel, who was a witness to the deed. That's logical, isn't it?'

Toby shook his head: 'Not very. Christabel swore that she hadn't seen anyone do anything.'

'Yes, but I don't take much account of that. She might have had her own reasons for protecting the murderer.'

'I quite agree, but whatever those reasons were they would have been just as valid three days later. The dilemma is this: if one of the Robinsons killed the old man and then heard Christabel categorically deny that she knew anything about it, they either believed her or they didn't. If they did, they had no cause to change their minds. If not, and they deemed it necessary to silence her permanently, then they'd have done so straight away. There were dozens of opportunities for the quick strike when she was alone in her cottage. Why wait till they'd got her under lock and key at the hospital?'

'Not very efficient locks and key, as it turned out.'

'Nevertheless, it involved extra risks and made it forty times more difficult. I don't mean to depress you, because I'm on your side, really.'

'I know that, and you don't depress me all that much, because I'm getting resigned to running into dead ends. Also I can point to a flaw in this particular argument. As I see it, the reason why Christabel was a danger after she got to the hospital, and not before, was because the word had got around that she was asking to see me. Until then, the murderer had been quite cosy in his fool's paradise, but he concluded that she'd had a change of heart and was going to spill the beans. Of course, you and I know that wasn't her intention at all. It was purely a private matter between me and her that she wanted to thrash out, but the murderer wasn't to know that. So we're left with this, Toby: the real murderer must be someone whom Sir Maddox had a hold over and who believed that Christabel possessed damning evidence against him – or her, come to that. Also, someone good at disguises.'

'Oh, really? False moustaches, dark glasses and so on?'

'Not to mention white coats and so on.'

'I see! A bit of a daredevil, wasn't he?'

'Yes, and we must be, too. I mean to go on prodding, until one of them gives himself away, cost what it may.'

'You'll have to prod fast, old girl. I don't think Robin has much intention of staying on here, once the inquest is in the bag.'

'Yes, only twenty-four hours. There's a lot to be done in the time, but first things first is my motto.'

'A good one. What are they?'

'A call on Mr Evans, followed by a nice cup of tea and a chat with O'Malley at the Mitre Hotel. Care to join us?'

SEVENTEEN

'DOLORES has been found,' Robin announced, a few hours later.

'And with a tale to unfold, to judge by your expression. Where?'

'Newhaven. Hadn't got very far, had she? But she had to wait around for a passage. It's not too easy to get them on demand, at this time of year, and she's a bit gormless.'

'Well, there must be more to it than that; otherwise, why would you be looking like Aunt Moo when the patience comes out without any cheating?'

'Oh yes, the patience has come out, with no cheating at all. Though only because the silly girl tried to travel on a false passport. Quite unnecessary, I need hardly say. She had a perfect right to leave the country whenever she chose, and once we'd established that she had no hand in the murder there weren't any real grounds to detain her. However, she's a bit dim and she probably thought the Harper Barringtons would raise a stink and have her forcibly brought back.'

'Which they did, presumably?'

'Oh no, they didn't. We had a watch out for her at ports and so on, as a matter of routine. After all, when someone disappears from a house where a murder has just been committed, it's bound to arouse a certain curiosity, isn't it?'

'But since you've said that she wasn't involved?'

'Aha! But that's not the whole story. People don't furnish themselves with false passports every time they cross the Channel, unless they're up to something. It was a lucky break for us, because it gave us all the excuse we needed to haul her in.'

'So what is the story? Come on, now, Robin! Oh, you can't, by any chance, mean . . . ?'

'Oh, but I can, my love. Our first little link in the art-theft chain. Isn't that spiffing?'

'It certainly is, and congratulations! All the same, it's hard to see what earthly use Dolores would have been to them. Apart from being dim, she could hardly speak a word of English.'

'She didn't need to. This is quite a cosmopolitan setup, by the sound of it. Besides, she was only a tiny cog in their machine; one of several who were planted in the neighbourhood to seek out potential quarries. Her job was simply to report on which families were going abroad, what arrangements had been made about caretakers and so on. Maria, in her innocence, was a great help there. She's been around these parts for ages and is well in with all the local domestics, particularly Dolly, who is a mine of information, all on her own.'

'But Maria is a goodie?'

'Oh yes; Dolores was vehement about that. It appears that she was completely taken in by Dolores and was very kind to her. Dolores had spun some hard-luck tale about a deserting husband, and Maria got her the job here by pretending that they came from the same village in Spain. That's a favourite way of planting these agents; by sheltering them under the credentials of some honest and soft-hearted compatriot. In fact, Dolores had been fired from her previous job for petty pilfering, which made her excellent fodder for the organisation.'

'So who was her contact? She must have been in touch with someone?'

'Just a telephone number. She had to call in between six and seven, once a week, whether there was anything to report or not. It was a set of numbers which she could dial, so she had no means of telling where it was situated.'

'And that was all she could tell you?'

'It will be enough. We'll get them now, all right; or some of them, at any rate. And, if she does know any more, Cole will soon shake it out of her. She'd popped a couple of Nancy's brooches in her reticule, just to make everything doubly easy for us, and she's scared silly, poor wretch,' Robin said, not sounding very sorry about it.

'And did she skip on instructions, or was that her own idea?'

'Her own entirely. She got the wind up when the police came swarming round, lost her head and bolted; for which I shall always be extremely grateful.'

'Perhaps you should be grateful to Christabel, as well?' I suggested.

He looked amused: 'I hadn't thought of it, but I suppose you're right. She flushed out my first little bird for me. Incidentally, I hope your remark implies that you're becoming reconciled to her guilt, because I'm afraid there's not much doubt about how the inquest will go tomorrow. Cole will do his level best to keep the publicity down to a minimum, if that's any consolation to you.'

'Not much, but I'm truly glad that everything has turned out so well, from your point of view. I suppose, if things go out as you expect, you plan to go back to London straight away?'

'May as well. There's nothing more to be done at this end. How about you? I don't suppose you're desperately keen to stick around, after what's happened?'

'I am not sure that being in London would make me feel any more cheerful. And, after all, Robin, you did apply for a few days' leave, which you've spent entirely on work. You've hardly had any time for your nice golfing.'

Robin was visibly impressed by this reminder and he said thoughtfully:

'Yes, that's very true; and, on the whole, I'm pleased to find that you are not in a tearing hurry to leave.'

'Are you, indeed? And why's that?'

'Well,' he said, 'the fact is, the Coles have invited us to supper on Thursday evening. I turned it down, because I thought you'd hate it. Now I can tell him it's on.'

EIGHTEEN

AT ELEVEN the following morning, there was an inquest on Christabel's death, immediately following a second one on Sir Maddox's. Both verdicts turned out precisely as Robin had predicted and an atmosphere of suppressed jubilation swept through the households concerned.

I do not think any of the inmates would have gone so far as to give a party to celebrate the outcome, but Anabel's seventeenth birthday was made the excuse.

Her mother, understandably, felt unequal to holding it at the Maltings, particularly as Dolores' defection had left her shorthanded; but Guy, who was the moving spirit in this enterprise, said that Och weel, it was a shame the puir wee lahsie shouldna have a wee bit of fun on her bairthday and that he and Xenia would gie a wee gahthering over at their place.

The highlight of this festivity was not to be a film show, but charades. Guy explained that this would help to start the ball rolling and to disperse any little constraints that might be hanging around, but I had not a doubt in the world that the main attraction was the chance to grab all the star rôles for himself.

As before, I went ahead with Aunt Moo and Harbart and, as before, the door was opened to us by Maria, the Russian steam-roller having miraculously stampeded Nancy into lending her for the evening.

The Robinsons' place was a flat over the Treasure Trove, formerly inhabited by the Nicholls family, traces of whose tenancy still remained in the flickering electric logs in the sitting-room fireplace and the acid-green tiles which surrounded it. In other respects the room resembled nothing so much as an extension of the shop below, and was crammed from floor to ceiling with antique furniture and ornaments. Few of them served any useful purpose, most were rather dusty and some still had price tags attached. This was a paradise for Aunt Moo, who padded round, asking Xenia how much she had paid for everything and then telling her she had been done for.

Our two contingents were the first to arrive and, with only six of us present, the room was already bursting at the seams. With the arrival, a few minutes afterwards, of two female Harper Barringtons, suffocation point was reached.

Nancy informed all her dears that Roger was most frantically sorry, but he had been detained in London on business and would be unable to join us until after dinner. This news brought some relief, although even without him it was hard to see how space could be found for a game of tiddliwinks, let alone charades.

I mentioned this to Guy and he explained that the spontaneous nature of the affair had only enabled him to clear one room and that the performances, as well as supper, would be held in the dining-room.

'This 'ere,' he continued, 'being as what you might call the communal dressing-room. Costumes, etcetera being in that there oak chest, as what your 'ubby is at present reclining on. And nah, ladies and gents, seeing as we're hall hassembled, ah baht a bit of a booze up?'

Laughing hysterically, to show Anabel what a good time we were having at her party, we traipsed after him into the adjoining room. Sure enough, it was a desert, by comparison. Apart from a sofa, with its back to the fireplace and representing the auditorium, there was a kitchen chair, a small table and assorted cushions in the centre of the room, which was to be the stage, and a long narrow table against the wall nearest the door. This was spread with slabs of cold chicken and mountains of Russian salad, which I considered to be taking chauvinism too far, and the whole being described by Toby in a gloomy undertone as *assiette angoisse*. Nor was he noticeably cheered by the sight of twelve bottles of glorious Algerian wine.

In contrast to all this, the glass and cutlery were of the highest order, having doubtless been borrowed from stock. There was crested Georgian silver and nine exquisite tumblers, each adorned with a gold laurel leaf encircling a different initial. Guy told me that they were part of a set of twenty-four, with the letters K and X left out. They had picked them up in a sale in Yorkshire, believing them to be French and very valuable, but had almost immediately decided that they could not bear to part with them. He said that they always brought them out for parties, where they made what he called a conversation piece. I could see that they also had a practical value, which had doubtless appealed to Xenia, in creating a one-man one-glass situation, throughout the evening and cutting the washing-up to a minimum.

On this occasion, Xenia was given the Z, which was no doubt customary, and I had to make do with P for Price, since there were two of us whose first name began with T.

At the conclusion of the glass ceremony, Guy took the floor again and outlined the programme for us. He said that we must divide into two teams and was immediately interrupted by Nancy, stipulating that it would be quite unfair if he and I were on the same side, and by Aunt Moo and Xenia, insisting in unison that they would take no active part, preferring to lend impartial support to each team in turn. This was a great relief to the rest of us, as one could well imagine them both talking far into the night, without ever bringing out the required syllable, or even getting around to a subject remotely related to it.

These matters settled, Guy told us that each side would have one turn, after which there would be an interval for supper, followed by a return match. He added that this would give more chance for Roger to arrive while there was still something to eat.

'Frightfully sweet of you, my dear,' Nancy informed him, 'but please don't put yourself out. One does so hate to be a nuisance, and I've left just a tiny snack of oysters and champagne for him at home, so he won't absolutely starve.'

This inspired Aunt Moo to throw out a few remarks concerning her preference for stout with oysters, causing Nancy's lip to curl, Xenia to announce that all beer was poison to the system, Anabel to dissolve into stifled giggles and Guy to clap his hands and call for order. We then picked sides, and he chose Anabel and Robin, while I got Nancy and Toby. I called Heads and lost and Guy, raring to go, led his party outside.

The word they chose was 'flatten', which wasn't bad, although not good enough to get past Toby, who had caught on long before the denouement. In the first scene, Guy was a Jewish estate-agent, with a bowler hat and a thick lisp. Robin and Anabel, the latter with all teeth humanely liberated for this festive occasion, played a nervous married couple, looking for a house and being repeatedly urged to take a flat instead; and, somewhere around this point, a memory began hammering itself out in my head.

In the next act Guy was a cockney bookmaker, shouting the odds in a check cap, and Robin and Anabel were a nervous married couple, who could not decide which horse to back. One way and another, the word ten got in about forty times.

In the final scene, Robin had become a nervous doctor, but Anabel broke out of the matrimonial rut and played a flighty nurse, with a handkerchief wrapped round her head. Guy also had a handkerchief round his head, to represent a bandage, and played a garrulous Pakistani, who had been knocked down by a lorry.

Watching them both, I was struck by a curious phenomenon and, simultaneously by my second revelation of the evening.

In recognition of her birthday, it fell to Anabel's honour to speak the whole word, which she managed to do, after much giggling and writhing, by saying: 'Now, now, you must lie flat; oh, sorry, I mean flatten out.' Whereupon, metaphorically speaking, the curtain came down.

'Did you notice what I noticed?' I muttered, joining Toby by the window, and turning my back on the room:

'Funny resemblance, you mean?'

'Amazing, isn't it? Looking at them now, one is staggered at having missed it. Of course, their tops are different. She's got a bulgy forehead, like her mother; but, when all you can see are those matching displays of teeth, it's unmistakable.'

'Does it give him a motive, according to your book?'

I considered the question in silence, until he repeated it.

'Honestly, Toby, it's a fair teaser. I had another idea about it, earlier on. Now I can't decide which of them to follow up.'

'Come on, chaps, no slacking!" Guy called out, behind us. 'No one gets fed till he's done his piece, you know.'

'You'll have to shelve them both,' Toby said, as we drifted towards the door. 'I have a nasty feeling that we're on.'

He was all for us using 'into' as the word, since it was practically impossible to guess, but Nancy said it would not be fair, and I backed her up. We eventually settled for 'monkey', which was rather a cheat, because we used the *k* twice over.

I shall skip the details of our first playlet, because they had no bearing on events; and, to be truthful, they now elude me completely. I presume that I did not acquit myself particularly well, for I went through the performance mechanically, three-quarters of my mind concentrating fiercely on matters right outside the game. The big surprise, which penetrated even this absorption, was provided by Nancy. She revealed a remarkable poise, plus genuine acting talent, and it was obvious that she held five-sixths of her audience in rapt attention. The exception was Robin, who stared stonily at a point somewhere over my left shoulder, occasionally casting his eyes up to the ceiling, as though in direct communication with a celestial informant.

This unsuspected skill of Nancy's caused me to wonder how much acting went into her everyday life and, during the first interval, I asked her whether she had ever been on the stage.

She was pulling a dusty black evening dress over her head, as I spoke, having been cast as a lady violinist, about to rehearse with Toby, the mad conductor. Her face emerged from its folds looking flushed and annoyed, and with chignon slightly askew.

'Not so's you'd notice, my dear. I did a few seasons in rep. before I married, but I was never in your class. By the way, Toby, which piece are we supposed to be doing?'

They settled for a Mozart concerto, and I entered left, seated myself on the kitchen chair and thumped out a few chords on the table, which had now become a Bechstein.

I had my back to the door throughout this scene, but when we were half-way through I heard a sound behind me. Sneaking a backward look, I saw that Roger had joined us. He was perched on one end of the dining-table and he winked at me and put a finger to his lips, when I turned round.

Nancy and Toby went into their final slanging-match, at the end of which she burst into a storm of realistic sobs. There was loud applause and Roger walked down stage and over the footlights, shouting 'Bravo!' and smiting Nancy a mighty blow between the shoulder blades, as he passed.

It was in the final scene that I received my third inspiration. I was supposed to be a schoolboy being escorted round Hampton Court by his irate grand-parents, when the bolt descended from the blue, and I abruptly switched nationalities and departed from the prepared script by shrilling out:

'Gee whiz, Granpaw, guess what? I just found this key. Think it could be the key to the maze, Granpaw?'

The other two looked understandably nonplussed, since we had already done the key bit in the previous scene, and some of their bafflement transmitted itself to the audience. I saw Guy and Anabel, side by side like two peas in a pod, gaping at me with identical toothy expressions, and Robin transferred his attention from the ceiling to bestow an icy stare in my direction, possibly on account of the hideously over-done American accent. Undaunted, I ad libbed away like a mad thing.

'Gosh, isn't that great, Granpaw and Granmaw? And lookee here,' I piped, holding out an empty hand. 'Look what else I found! Isn't it real cute?'

Old Granpaw had caught on by this time and he said that it most certainly was, and I was a smart kid. He then raised his eyebrows and, when I shook my head, gave Nancy the prearranged cue. She informed me flatly that I was a tiresome young monkey, who would be sent straight upstairs to its bedroom, and the play fizzled out into silence.

Robin and Guy made a dutiful pretence of being unable to guess the word, until elucidation burst upon Anabel; whereupon Guy jumped up and commanded everyone to partake of a nosh-up.

Xenia doled out dollops of chicken and salad and Guy topped up the glasses, which Maria brought round on a tray. This was an embarrassment, on every count, because I had no hands left and the wine tasted of warm stewed plums. Seeing my fix, Robin picked up my glass and placed it behind the curtain, on the window sill.

'Cheer up!' I whispered, handing a plate to Aunt Moo. 'Who knows? There may be some lovely hot soup for us when we get home?'

I got a very beady look in return for this, and she advised me to look at my step, as curiosity had been known to kill the goose. It was all I needed.

When everyone had been attended to and all but me were unhappily balancing a plate in one hand and a glass in the other, we stood to attention while Guy led off a glee-club version of 'Happy Birthday'. Timing it simultaneously, Robin and I waited for the 'dear Aa-na . . . bel' bit, then lunged forward from opposite sides of the room and knocked the glass from Toby's hand.

The wine spilled out over the carpet, he was spattered from head to foot with Russian salad, and he looked most aggrieved:

'Not so hasty, please!' he grumbled. 'You surely didn't imagine I was going to drink it?'

Nineteen

'I MADE numerous mistakes,' I said, 'which I freely acknowledge.'

'Splendid!' Toby said. 'And this would be the moment.'

'Four in all,' I went on, doing some calculations. 'I shall begin with the last.'

'Naturally,' Robin said.

'Because that one wasn't entirely my fault, you see. I confess I was to blame in not keeping you informed of my progress, but that was because I thought you would stamp on me. If you had only dropped a hint that you weren't satisfied with the verdict, we could have worked as a team and probably got the answer twice as quickly.'

'I am thankful you didn't, though,' Toby said. 'Your acting separately practically knocked me insensible and ruined a perfectly good suit. One trembles to think what you might have accomplished as a team.'

'And my dissatisfaction, as Tessa calls it, was too nebulous to be worth passing on, with everything pointing the other way. I suppose you could say that your summing-up of Christabel's character and the conflict between that and what she was supposed to have done made a stronger impression on me than it was wise to let on, in view of the mountain of evidence against you.'

'How can you say that? It was seeing the way you carried on during those ghastly charades which gave me the boost I needed.'

'Carried on?'

'Don't deny it, Robin. You weren't even pretending to enter into the spirit, either with those feeble performances of yours, or when you were supposed to be guessing. And that's so unlike you. The only time you go *distrait* is when you're not sure of the form. So what was there for you to be uncertain about at that stage, I asked myself; and the answer came pretty promptly.'

'Oh, good! And I hope you will promptly pass it on to me.'

I concluded, from his sour expression, that the Algerian wine was giving him trouble.

'No, it suddenly struck me that the reason why he had consented to go to that awful party, and pass up our date with the Coles and everything, was because it gave him a last chance to study all those people in one gathering and maybe pick up something he missed. Isn't that so, Robin?'

'There may be a grain of truth in it. I was afraid the sacrifice would be wasted, though, when it looked as though our man wasn't going to turn up.'

'I know; and being so late was a bad blunder on his part. Even if the plan hadn't miscarried completely, he would only have succeeded in poisoning the wrong person.'

'Though I doubt if we'd have pinned it on him, since the motive was non-existent. On the other hand; I suppose it would have been that much harder for him to make a third attempt.'

'Third?' Toby repeated.

'Oh, this was the second crack he'd had at poor old Tessa. The first was when he tried to break her skull, in Christabel's barn. He might have got away with it, too, if Christabel hadn't seen him first and shouted a warning, which caused Tessa to turn her head just enough to deflect his aim.'

'When did you work that one out?' I asked.

'During an interview I had with Mr Harper Barrington, after his arrest,' Robin said smoothly. 'I am sorry you were not invited to be present, but Cole is a stickler for the correct procedures.'

'Oh, very funny! Did Roger shoot Prince, as well?'

'Yes. The Robinsons were supposed to be taking care of him, because Roger was always threatening to have him put down, unless he was kept under control, but he escaped and followed his old, unloving master. There was no shaking him off apparently, and Roger was afraid he would ruin his plan. He'd been out shooting in the Haverford woods and he spied Tessa walking along the bridle path. So he stayed out of sight and kept an eye on her. Then he saw the constable ride off and that gave him a heaven-sent chance. Unfortunately for him, he was at such pains to keep behind the barn and out of sight that he missed Christabel's arrival in the taxi. His plan was to creep round and enter by the stable door, but Prince was rather undisciplined, as you know, and gave every sign of rushing ahead and barking. So Roger called him off, retreated a few hundred yards into the paddock and shot him through the head. After which, he came back to finish the job on Tessa; but he had reckoned without Christabel, of course. It's hard to see how he could have found still another opportunity, so, if you had drunk the poisoned wine, Toby, you would have died in a good cause.'

'Thank you. I shall try to remember that, although there was never the faintest risk. I had no intention of drinking the horrid stuff.'

'I couldn't rely on that, and I was almost certain it was in your glass. Anyone arriving at the party when Roger did would automatically assume that Tessa had been given the T initial. All the same, I had to get her glass away from her first, just in case I'd miscalculated.'

'I am so grateful to you for putting me first, Robin, but I had come to roughly the same conclusions.'

'And, so far, it seems to be all self-congratulation,' Toby complained. 'It is rather disappointing. I thought we were going to hear about some of Tessa's mistakes.'

'And so you shall. The principal one was my assumption that Christabel wanted to see me to confess about Mott's pictures not being by him at all. It was idiotic of me, because there was really no need for it. I already knew, and she had guessed that I knew, so what was left to say?'

'But why did she want to see you, then?'

'For exactly the reason the murderer worked out. She knew that an attempt had been made on my life and she wanted to warn me. I expect she was too doped at first, to know what was what, and later she went out of action with a heart attack. I take it that was genuine, by the way?'

'Yes, it was,' Roger assured me, 'and it must have seemed like a terrific break for Roger, don't you think? With a little bit of luck, she'd have died a natural death and saved him a heap of trouble.'

'In some ways, I wish she had, poor old thing; but when she recovered she must have had a lucid period and remembered what had happened. She probably even recognised my attacker.'

'That's more doubtful.'

'Why?'

'Because if she could identify him why should she then have allowed him to walk into her room at the hospital, without raising the alarm?'

'Yes, that puzzled me at first. I worked out all sorts of theories about his putting on a white coat and disguising himself as a porter, but now I believe he used a much simpler device. The point is –'

'The point, in my opinion,' Toby interrupted, 'is that it made no difference whether she recognised him in the barn or not. I am certain she knew all along who had killed Sir Brands Hatch.'

I nodded: 'Me, too. I think Roger sat them together at the film show, believing her to be scatty and half-blind, and therefore the safest person, from his point of view. If you remember, Nancy began by taking that place for herself, but Roger made her change over. What he didn't know was that Christabel was wearing her reading-glasses that evening. She'd left home in a hurry and picked up the wrong pair. So it was the screen which was out of her vision, not the things which were going on within inches of her nose. It put her in a first-class position to see the murderer at work, and it also meant that she was never at any moment diverted by the sight of Nancy prancing around on the poop deck.'

'Then, if it's true and she really did see everything,' Robin said sadly, 'I am afraid she got her just desserts. Accessory to murder is a serious crime.'

'Oh yes, but there's nothing to be done about it now; and Christabel always made her own rules. It's my belief that she knew Roger had killed the old man, but it suited her book to have him out of the way, and she probably wished she'd had the guts to do it herself. That being so, I expect she told Roger she wouldn't give him away, so long as he didn't get up to any more tricks.'

'Then it was highly immoral of her, and remarkably naive, if you'll allow me to say so.'

'I do allow you to say so, Robin, darling, because it's true. She was naive, and immoral, too, by general standards. Also, she never learnt that other people didn't necessarily play the game by her rules. But she stuck to them herself, and it was jolly bad luck for Roger that she happened to be present when I got my clump on the head.'

'And what had you done to make him so keen to murder you?' Toby asked me.

'He must have been afraid I had found him out, or was on the brink of doing so. It's funny about Roger. I always thought of him as rather an ass, but in some respects he was a jump ahead. He saw that I had bumped up against his motive, even before I saw it myself. I was fooled by that boisterous Battle of Britain manner, but one ought to remember that people don't make vast piles on the Stock Exchange simply by twirling their moustaches.'

'But what made him believe that you were about to unmask him?'

'Well, he was wary of me right from the start, I dare say, because I told him I was doing some Teach Yourself Company Law and so on. Quite untrue, as it happened, but I am apt to get carried away, and he fell for it. When I started shrieking about his cute little bar, the next morning, he must have thought I was really creeping up on him, although that was quite inadvertent, too.'

'Why did that ring the alarm bells?' Toby asked. 'I realise the word had some dreaded significance for him; hence your lapse into gibberish in the charade game, but I still haven't gathered what the significance was.'

'Which reminds me,' Robin said. 'That act of yours was an unnecessary trimming, you know. I had already seen him drop something into one of the glasses, even though I wasn't sure which.'

'Yes, but I had my back to him when he first came in. My intention was to jostle him into making some stupid move by showing clearly that I was on to him. How could I know that he'd already made the stupid move? You see, Toby, he was up to his neck in some shady deal with a certain Mr Flatmore in the States, who had been kicked out of a company called Consolidated United Trust Enterprises when one of his smart take-overs fell flat on its face. I don't have to spell it out for you, do I? You know how these high-powered people love making funny words out of sets of initials? Presumably, this Flatmore and Roger had been cooking up a similar deal in this country and, when the crash came, Roger was landed with about two million worthless shares. I expect he could have slithered out of it, given time, but that was probably the one thing which Sir Maddox wouldn't give him.'

'So you think Sir Mad had uncovered this shady plot?'

'Yes. In fact, Roger was so anxious to curry favour in that quarter that it wouldn't surprise me if he had tipped Maddox off to buy a few shares, too; letting him in on the ground floor and all that jazz. Even that might have been sorted out, with Maddox safely larking round Russia for another five or six weeks, but his pictures were stolen and he came zooming back to London. I don't suppose he was in any mood to turn the other cheek when he discovered that Roger had landed him in a dud financial deal. Probably, threats of exposure were being flung around in all directions. Even if Roger had escaped prosecution for fraud, he'd have been pretty well ruined, and we all know how little that would have appealed to him.'

'Yes, you've more or less summed it up,' Robin agreed. 'It was useless for him to deny it, once his business affairs had been investigated. He's pleading guilty, by the way.'

'Poor old Nancy and Anabel! They're the ones I feel sorry for.'

'In a sense, it's not half so bad for Anabel, though, is it?'

'I suppose not. Tell me something; were Nancy and Guy ever married?'

'Yes, briefly. They met in a summer show in Brighton. She was about eighteen and wildly impressed, I dare say, by all his name-dropping. Then she got pregnant, and he was out of work, and the marriage broke up. She went back to her parents, until Roger rode up on his white charger. He took the child on as well, but Nancy seems always to have resented her. Guy, in the meantime, had married Xenia and retired into the antiques business, although, as you have discovered, he wasn't too choosy about where the stock came from. It was sheer fluke that he and Nancy eventually landed up in the same village; though, given their later careers, one could say that Burleigh was a typical sort of background for both of them. And neither Roger nor Xenia was the type to be dislodged by such a poor little skeleton in the cupboard as Anabel. Cole dug this up, but naturally, he only passed it on to me in the strictest confidence.'

'And, for once, Tessa, I think you must admit he was right. If Robin had let you into those secrets, I can just see you going all out to pin the murder on Guy, the long-lost, avenging father. It would have fitted your novelettish view of life.'

'I might remind you that it was my novelettish view of life which made me insist on Christabel's innocence, and that can't be bad.'

'However, you never managed to find out how Roger persuaded her to swallow the poison,' Robin said. 'So far, he's only been charged with one murder, which will do to be going on with.'

'No need to go on with it for long, though. O'Malley and I have got it all straightened out. In the first place, he did it by remote control and the wheels had been set in motion long before she sent the message asking for me. I believe that he had only pretended to play along with her, when she issued her ultimatum and he never really trusted her to keep her mouth shut. I expect he'd have found a simpler method of killing her, but the fire, and her being in hospital, forced his hand.'

'Forced his hand to what?'

'I must explain that, on the day after the fire, I called at the hospital to leave some flowers. She wasn't allowed visitors, but heaps of people had rung up and sent things. Among them was a whacking great hamper, with the Harper Barringtons' card on it; and what do you suppose was included, along with the peaches and grapes? Some dear little boxes of chewing-gum. Wasn't that brilliant? He guessed that she wouldn't be allowed to smoke and would inevitably run out of cigarettes, in any case; and he also knew, as we all did, about her habit of swallowing gum practically whole, during these crises.'

'Your theory being that the poison was in the gum? Everything of that kind was analysed, but the results were all negative.'

'The whole plan would have hinged on its being in only one piece. The only way you could have found it was by analysing everything before she died, and nobody thought of that.'

'I suppose it could have been injected into the gum,' Robin admitted slowly. 'Only such a minute quantity would have been needed.'

'And there were masses of chemicals and instruments down in the cellar. Mr Evans says all you'd need is a syringe and a steady hand. Roger could have practised it for as long as he liked. Besides, Christabel was far too careless and shortsighted to notice if one piece of gum had got a bit mangled.'

Robin stood up: 'I couldn't guarantee it, but I think you may have got something. I'd better talk to Cole. The Maltings was searched, inside and out, including that famous Hobbies Room, but it might be worth taking another look.'

'That's how it is nowadays,' I sighed, when he had gone. 'Not a word of thanks, you notice. All he thinks about is bringing comfort and cheer to silly old Cole.'

'Well, I expect he likes to feel he is taking some active part. You seem to have left him so little to do.'

'Oh, nonsense, Toby! You make me sound too bossy for words. Besides, he's done the job he came here to do, and that's what counts. The murders were just an unforeseen complication. Although, to be frank, I do think Cole's method of poring over statements and fingerprints is rather a waste of time. It doesn't get you anywhere, when you're up against a bunch like this.'

'Perhaps they should disband the police force, after all? Hand the whole thing over to such members of the theatrical profession who happen to be resting?'

'Well, at least my enforced rest enabled me to pay attention to Aunt Moo's words of wisdom.'

'Is that what they're called?'

'Admittedly, not always the right words in the right place, but she's as shrewd as they come, and if you spend enough time on it you soon begin to tune in. Incidentally, I suppose you're not worried about your inheritance being systematically whittled away, down at the Treasure Trove?'

'Not at all. I'm in favour of her having an interesting hobby for her declining years. Also, to be quite truthful, Tessa, she's making mincemeat of those Robinsons. I happen to know that she's unloading all the junk on them and getting the most inflated prices. I should never be surprised if my capital were increasing by leaps and bounds.'

'So there you are! It confirms what I was saying. She was always telling us that Xenia didn't know a fig about antiques and paid far too much for everything. Uncle Mad said it, too, by the way, but he overstated the case by hinting that the shop was a cover-up for something criminal. He hinted it to all and sundry, though, so there was no point in murdering him to shut him up. The rumour had got around, whether true or not. Aunt Moo knew it wasn't, of course, and she also knew something about Maddox which was worth waiting for. When I got the message, I never looked back.'

'Good heavens! Whatever can it have been?'

'She said he was a very curious man and, furthermore that he was curious about a lot of other things as well as pictures. As a matter of fact, the word was inquisitive, and when I understood that it gave me a different view of things. Until then we'd been bogged down in the belief that paintings and art thefts were at the root of this murder; but then I began asking myself what secret, discreditable knowledge he might have dug up, which had no connection with such things. Roger was an obvious starting point, because he was Top of the Get Rich Quick League, and people who adore money and spend their time amassing it are apt to be vulnerable.'

'That's really most interesting,' Toby said thoughtfully. 'And, honestly, Tessa, I have the strongest feeling that you should tell Robin about this. No doubt, he would have preferred to solve the case all by himself, but it may come as balm to the wounds to know that it is not you he has to thank, but Aunt Moo.'

'You are absolutely right,' I agreed. 'I was coming to the same conclusion, myself. And you never know, Toby. Between us, we might just be able to convince him that he'd have caught on himself if he'd ever understood a single word she uttered.'

THE END

FELICITY SHAW

THE detective novels of Anne Morice seem rather to reflect the actual life and background of the author, whose full married name was Felicity Anne Morice Worthington Shaw. Felicity was born in the county of Kent on February 18, 1916, one of four daughters of Harry Edward Worthington, a well-loved village doctor, and his pretty young wife, Muriel Rose Morice. Seemingly this is an unexceptional provenance for an English mystery writer—yet in fact Felicity's complicated ancestry was like something out of a classic English mystery, with several cases of children born on the wrong side of the blanket to prominent sires and their humbly born paramours. Her mother Muriel Rose was the natural daughter of dressmaker Rebecca Garnett Gould and Charles John Morice, a Harrow graduate and footballer who played in the 1872 England/Scotland match. Doffing his football kit after this triumph, Charles became a stockbroker like his father, his brothers and his nephew Percy John de Paravicini, son of Baron James Prior de Paravicini and Charles' only surviving sister, Valentina Antoinette Sampayo Morice. (Of Scottish mercantile origin, the Morices had extensive Portuguese business connections.) Charles also found time, when not playing the fields of sport or commerce, to father a pair of out-of-wedlock children with a coachman's daughter, Clementina Frances Turvey, whom he would later marry.

Her mother having passed away when she was only four years old, Muriel Rose was raised by her half-sister Kitty, who had wed a commercial traveler, at the village of Birchington-on-Sea, Kent, near the city of Margate. There she met kindly local doctor Harry Worthington when he treated her during a local measles outbreak. The case of measles led to marriage between the physician and his patient, with the couple wedding in 1904, when Harry was thirty-six and Muriel Rose but twenty-two. Together Harry and Muriel Rose had a daughter, Elizabeth, in 1906. However Muriel Rose's three later daughters—Angela, Felicity and Yvonne—were fathered by another man, London playwright Frederick Leonard Lonsdale, the author of such popular stage works (many of them adapted as films) as *On Approval* and *The Last of Mrs. Cheyney* as well as being the most steady of Muriel Rose's many lovers.

Unfortunately for Muriel Rose, Lonsdale's interest in her evaporated as his stage success mounted. The playwright proposed pensioning off his discarded mistress with an annual stipend of one hundred pounds apiece for each of his natural daughters, provided that he and Muriel Rose never met again. The offer was accepted, although Muriel Rose, a woman of golden flights and fancies who romantically went by the name Lucy Glitters (she told her daughters that her father had christened her with this appellation on account of his having won a bet on a horse by that name on the day she was born), never got over the rejection. Meanwhile, "poor Dr. Worthington" as he was now known, had come down with Parkinson's Disease and he was packed off with a nurse to a cottage while "Lucy Glitters," now in straitened financial circumstances by her standards, moved with her daughters to a maisonette above a cake shop in Belgravia, London, in a bid to get the girls established. Felicity's older sister Angela went into acting for a profession, and her mother's theatrical ambition for her daughter is said to have been the inspiration for Noel Coward's amusingly imploring 1935 hit song "Don't Put Your Daughter on the Stage, Mrs. Worthington." Angela's greatest contribution to the cause of thespianism by far came when she married actor and theatrical agent Robin Fox, with whom she produced England's Fox acting dynasty, including her sons Edward and James and grandchildren Laurence, Jack, Emilia and Freddie.

Felicity meanwhile went to work in the office of the GPO Film Unit, a subdivision of the United Kingdom's General Post Office established in 1933 to produce documentary films. Her daughter Mary Premila Boseman has written that it was at the GPO Film Unit that the "pretty and fashionably slim" Felicity met documentarian Alexander Shaw—"good looking, strong featured, dark haired and with strange brown eyes between yellow and green"—and told herself "that's the man I'm going to marry," which she did. During the Thirties and Forties Alex produced and/or directed over a score of prestige documentaries, including *Tank Patrol*, *Our Country* (introduced by actor Burgess Meredith) and *Penicillin*. After World War Two Alex worked with the United Nations agencies UNESCO and UNRWA and he and Felicity and their three children resided in developing nations all around the world. Felicity's daughter Mary recalls that Felicity "set up house in most of these places adapting to each circumstance. Furniture and curtains and so on were made of local materials. . . . The only possession that followed us everywhere from England was the box of Christmas decorations, practically heirlooms, fragile and attractive and unbroken throughout. In Wad Medani in the Sudan they hung on a thorn bush and looked charming."

It was during these years that Felicity began writing fiction, eventually publishing two fine mainstream novels, *The Happy Exiles* (1956) and *Sun-Trap* (1958). The former novel, a lightly satirical comedy of manners about British and American expatriates in an unnamed British colony during the dying days of the Empire, received particularly good reviews and was published in both the United Kingdom and the United States, but after a nasty bout with malaria and the death, back in England, of her mother Lucy Glitters, Felicity put writing aside for more than a decade, until under her pseudonym Anne Morice, drawn from her two middle names, she successfully launched her Tessa Crichton mystery series in 1970. "From the royalties of these books," notes Mary Premila Boseman, "she was able to buy a house in Hambleden, near Henley-on-Thames; this was the first of our houses that wasn't rented." Felicity spent a great deal more time in the home country during the last two decades of her life, gardening and cooking for friends (though she herself when alone subsisted on a diet of black coffee and watercress) and industriously spinning her tales of genteel English murder in locales much like that in which she now resided. Sometimes she joined Alex in his overseas travels to different places, including Washington, D.C., which she wrote about with characteristic wryness in her 1977 detective novel *Murder with Mimicry* ("a nice lively book saturated with show business," pronounced the *New York Times Book Review*). Felicity Shaw lived a full life of richly varied experiences, which are rewardingly reflected in her books, the last of which was published posthumously in 1990, a year after her death at the age of seventy-three on May 18th, 1989.

Curtis Evans